NEW YORK NIGHTFALL

AN INTERNATIONAL DETECTIVE THRILLER

LUKE RICHARDSON

1

New York. Present Day.

THERE ARE moments in life when the present leaves the past behind. It's as though the sharp knife of a surgeon cuts one from the other. Things divide neatly at these moments. They reinvent themselves in a wave of paradigm-shifting realizations. The world turns on a different axis and the old 'you' stands there, motionless and watching, as the new 'you' walks out into the unknown.

He turned his face to the sky. Light rain peppered his skin. The wet swish of tires on asphalt sounded distant here. The city was quiet. He tightened his grip and the flow of blood slowed. The blood had streamed over his fingers, now, it barely even dribbled.

He gazed down at the woman. At her eyes, still, and like marbles. Her skin, smooth as satin. Her mouth, an expressionless circle. The gash in her neck was the only thing that proved to him she was not simply resting.

The knife had also separated him from his past self. He was now a killer. A murderer. *Her* murderer.

The blade felt cold between his fingers. He lifted it to his face. Although the dripping blood was barely visible in the shadows, he could smell it. It was nourishing and fresh, like rain in the jungle.

His tongue flicked out between wet lips.

He was suddenly alert. Voices echoed down the passageway.

"No, not like this," he hissed, his voice barely audible over the hammering rain.

He couldn't be discovered now. He needed time. He must have time to finish the job.

A group of people passed the passage's entrance on the road ahead. He watched them closely, his sense of exposure growing. It was as though the world, once again, was trying to take away what was his.

The intruders wandered on, their coats glistened beneath streetlights. One of them laughed, and the noise sounded sinister to him, standing over the body. He stood rigid for several long seconds—he couldn't tell exactly how many. When all the intruders had passed the passageway's opening, he breathed a sigh of relief. None looked down the passageway. It was as though he and the woman didn't exist. He chuckled to himself, the noise came out sounding more like the dry heave of a fuel-less engine. Why would anyone look down here? Margins of a city like this held no interest to predictable people like that. He laughed again. They probably wouldn't even notice the alleyway existed, nestled beside the bright lights of the building next door.

He glanced up at the side wall of the building now. It was, after all, the reason he had chosen this location to begin with. That building was Mansel Buck M.D.'s practice. Buck was the city's most prominent cosmetic surgeon. Those with fame and fortune passed through the brightly lit doors at the front of the building for a nip, tuck, or whatever else was in vogue right now.

Here in the shadows was no-man's-land.

The voices of the intruders faded away into the whisper of the city. He drew a breath. No one had seen him. That was good. Yet, he didn't have much time. Time remained the enemy here. Time had almost prevented his great-grandfather from fulfilling his artistic desires. He was determined that would not happen to him.

He pulled up his left sleeve and looked at his wrist. His great-grandfather's gold chain glinted beneath some distant light.

"This is for you," he whispered, placing the chain against his lips. It tasted like blood. "It's all for you."

Then he dropped to his knees and unbuttoned her coat. While he worked, he wondered what he should call her now that she was dead.

He never knew her name, anyway. He paused and thought for a moment, maybe he should find out. She probably had some identification in her bag or saved in her phone. Everyone had something nowadays. His hands dropped the coat, half undone, and he reached across to the handbag which was discarded on the concrete. He froze inches from the bag.

"No, this won't do," he muttered, focusing again on the body. "Time is of the essence. Time is the enemy."

Ultimately, he decided, it didn't matter who she was in life. That part of her was gone, and now she was his. Plus, he knew he would find out on the news tomorrow. The news station loved to drag up the entire history of the unfortunate, including their whole life story. Right now, he needed to focus; he needed to concentrate. There was work to do.

Moments like this were precious. He needed to make the

most of them. She had died so that he could have this time. He owed it to her sacrifice.

He slid his hands beneath her clothes and cursed the need to wear gloves. He wanted to feel her. To sense each ripple of her skin. Her body was still warm. That was good.

"The body," he corrected himself out loud. "She is *the body* now, as it no longer belonged to her."

If he were to be pedantic, he thought, then maybe he should call it *his body* now. He'd created it, after all.

He smiled.

He pulled at the raincoat, struggling to slide it from her limp arms with one hand. He put the knife down and used both hands to twist the raincoat from her. He thought of those mannequins in shops with removable arms and heads so they could be easily dressed. Maybe that's what he needed to do here.

He peered at the knife, blood dripping from the blade and fanning across the floor.

"Come on, come on," he whispered, weaving her limp arms from the sleeves.

The rain fell harder now. It ran from his face and inside his coat. It slipped over his back and chest. He didn't care. For a moment he thought of those rainy nights in London, all those years ago. It would have felt just like this. He smiled with excitement.

Her thick jumper was already wet. Water had soaked into her clothes when she fell. It didn't matter. He picked up the knife and slid it carefully inside the jumper. He didn't want to cut the skin. Yet.

He sliced through the fabric and peeled the garment away. He felt a flurry of excitement. *The body. His body.*

Blood from the ugly gash on her neck had run inside her clothes. He rubbed his hands through it. Blood smeared across her pale skin. She was cooling. He had to work quickly.

Then he heard it. It didn't sound like much against the drumming of the rain and murmur of the city, but it was enough to pull him from his trance.

His head whipped from left to right. Mansel Buck M. D's Cosmetic Surgery had closed hours ago. No one had any business coming down here tonight.

He heard it again. Movement. He turned and gazed back toward the street.

A figure cast a silhouette against the glaring lights of the road. It moved closer.

He sprung to his feet and turned.

The stooped figure slouched closer.

This was not part of the plan.

He gripped the knife. He could kill again, of course. But that wasn't the way things were done.

"Just trying to get out of the rain," the figure said. A murmuring singsong hissed through toothless gums. Words slurred by drugs or madness. "It'll be nice to get home. Get warm."

The figure sidled further into the alley. The intruder hadn't seen him yet.

He looked back at the body. *His body.*

Her pale skin glowed ethereally in the gloom. *An angel.*

He didn't want to give up his prize. She was beautiful but tainted now.

The ecstasy of the kill drained away. He couldn't get caught on the first one. That wasn't the way it was supposed to go.

Next time.

He pulled the hood of his raincoat low over his eyes,

concealed the knife within his sleeve, and pushed past the figure.

"Oh, sorry," the figure mumbled. "Just trying to get out of the rain."

He would have to start again. Then he would finish the job.

2

St Lucia, The Caribbean. Present Day.

THE ST LUCIAN closed in on the Caribbean Sea. The day had been calm but hot. It was precisely the sort of day the locals in the markets of Castries hated. Making their way home for dinner or a swift drink at the rum shop, they fanned the heat away with menus, newspapers, or even their fingers.

The pool at St James' Bay, which an hour before had been filled with the shouts and splashes of children, grew quiet with the dying day. The calm water rippled gently, reflecting the surrounding palm trees.

"Not bad at all," Leo said, glancing at Allissa, who was lying on the sun lounger beside him. Yet again, a strange sensation passed through him when he saw her in her red bikini.

"I could certainly get used to it," Allissa said, glancing at the tablet set up on the table between them. The screen showed the feed from a camera hidden in a bush on the access road to their target's mansion. All they had to do was note down who came and went, nothing more.

Allissa looked at the screen for a long moment and then turned her attention to the cocktail which sat beside the tablet. She snagged up the glass and tipped the remainder of the drink into her mouth.

"I'll get a refill," Leo said, climbing to his feet.

"Drinking on the job, you naughty boy," Allissa said playfully. She held out the empty glass for Leo to take. "If you insist."

"I think we're just about done here for the day," Leo said, nodding toward the screen. In the evenings they had set the system to record movement, which they could then log the following day. So far, all it had recorded was a troop of vervet monkeys who liked to run up and down the road for hours during the night.

"Why don't we just do jobs like this in the future," Allissa said, chuckling. "It's much easier than chasing bad guys."

"It's certainly not been as difficult as some of our other cases," Leo said, looking out at the sun, which was an hour from disappearing altogether. "Although I must commend you for your hardworking attitude to sun lounging. Most people gave up hours ago." Leo glanced at the other sun loungers, most of which were now empty.

"I'm always giving one hundred and ten percent," Allissa said, rolling over.

Leo padded across to the bar and ordered a refill. When the client had offered to fly them to the Caribbean, Allissa had suggested the all-inclusive. Usually whilst on the road, the pair favored local restaurants which put their money directly in the hands of the people who lived and worked there, but this once they had settled on a bit of luxury.

As the barman got to work, Leo stared up at the large screen behind the bar. A twenty-four-hour news channel recapped the day's headlines. Although not really paying attention, Leo's eyes were drawn to the screen. The news channel's logo flashed and then disappeared, showing a serious-looking anchorman.

Leo leaned forward, listening to the anchorman's words.

"Gabriel Marke has been identified as the prime suspect as the man behind an international drug ring," the anchorman said.

A picture of Gabriel Marke appeared on the screen. Leo's body went rigid, the easy languor of moments ago replaced by a steely tension. His gaze hardened and locked on the screen. His muscles tightened as if what he saw had wired him into a state of hyper-alertness.

Leo's mind raced. Every detail of Marke's face — a face he had memorized already — was so familiar that he could instantly recall it.

"Marke is suspected to have been behind a string of brutal murders stretching across the globe," the anchorman continued.

When the barman turned around with a drink in each hand, Leo was nowhere to be seen.

Leo ran through the resort and back to the poolside.

"It's him!" he shouted, reaching Allissa.

Allissa spun around and sat bolt upright.

"What? What's him?" She said, eyeing Leo in confusion.

"How could we be so stupid?" Leo groaned, his lips set in a grimace. "We should have checked more thoroughly." Leo paced six feet one way and then turned around and paced back.

"Okay, whatever you had in that drink, it's clearly not agreed with you," Allissa said, climbing to her feet. She intercepted Leo as he paced past again and grabbed him by the shoulders. "What's going on?"

Leo grabbed the tablet and ran an internet search for *Gabriel Marke*. A second later, various images of the man filled the screen. He handed the tablet to Allissa.

Allissa looked at the search results for several seconds. When she finally looked up at Leo, her features were etched with a quiet trepidation. The fear in her eyes was real and raw.

"The client lied to us," Leo muttered, loud enough so that Allissa could only just hear. "The man we're spying on is not her husband. It's Gabriel Marke, one of the most dangerous men on the planet."

"The camera equipment," Allissa said, grasping the tablet with both hands. "Is there any way he could trace that to us?" The pair locked eyes.

"Honestly, I don't know. I bought it online back in England. But it will have a serial number and..." Leo's response lodged in his throat. A strangled silence took hold as he tried to speak. A constricting band of apprehension tightened around his stomach, making each breath an effort.

"The internal storage," Leo said. "If they download the footage stored on the camera, they will see us driving away."

The pair locked eyes, as they realized the decision was made for them.

"We need to get that camera and then get off this island," Allissa said, her voice grave.

All Leo could do was nod.

Back on their hired bike, Leo and Allissa powered up the road which led toward Marke's mansion. The daylight was dying now, but the pair had decided they couldn't wait a single moment recovering their equipment.

Allissa slowed the engine as they reached the position where the camera was hidden. The roof of the mansion was just visible a few hundred feet further up the road. Seeing the building now sent a shudder of fear through Allissa's body. She could only imagine the horrors Marke performed within those walls.

Leo slipped off the back and stalked into the jungle. He found the camera quickly, slipped it into his bag, and returned to the bike. As he reached the road, another sound cut through the jungle. Another engine roared from nearby.

Leo's muscles tensed and his focus snapped to the winding road that led to Marke's lair. In a blur of motion, a Jeep roared into view, barreling around the corner with reckless abandon. Dust billowed as the vehicle shot forward.

With an urgent surge of adrenaline, Leo sprinted forward, the camera clenched in his grasp. He leapt onto the back of the bike. Allissa glanced back just long enough to ensure Leo was secure before slamming the throttle.

The bike roared to life, and with a fierce kickback of gravel and dust, they powered ahead. The dirt road beneath them became a blur as Allissa powered the bike back toward the town.

"It was all going so well!" Leo shouted, his arms clamped around Allissa's waist as she twisted the bike's throttle. The engine roared, as they tore down the narrow road.

"We should have known that things are never as simple as they seem," Allissa shouted over her shoulder, her voice almost lost in the wind that whipped her hair into a wild dance.

The guttural growl of the Jeep cut through the night.

Leo swung around and saw the vehicle tear around the corner. It was the sort of rugged all-terrain vehicle that was common in the Caribbean because of its ability to navigate the narrow and bumpy roads.

"Maybe we could just explain what we're doing there?" Leo shouted. The Jeep accelerated, closing the distance between them.

"Gabriel Marke is definitely not one to just let us explain," Allissa nodded backward.

"I think you're probably right," Leo said. Leo glanced over his shoulder and saw the Jeep pulling closer still. The driver snarled through the windscreen.

Allissa accelerated into a curve, gravel spitting up behind the tires. She leaned into the turn with a practiced ease. For a beat, the bike's rear tire skidded perilously, hunting for traction through the loose gravel. With a deft twist of control, Allissa mastered the slide, sending a spray of stones hurtling into the undergrowth.

Leo, clinging tightly to Allissa from behind, felt a jolt of adrenaline spike through him as the bike fishtailed. Undergrowth shot past in a blur, one tree almost slapping him around the face.

"Whatever that guy is up to," Allissa shouted, "he clearly doesn't like being watched."

"Thanks for stating the obvious," Leo said. The funny thing was, in the few days they had been watching the property, they had seen nothing particularly alarming. A few people came and went, but generally the place was quiet.

Reaching the end of the bend, Allissa hit the gas again, trying to increase their lead as much as possible. For a few seconds, the Jeep remained out of sight, and then slid around the corner behind them.

Leo twisted around, stealing a glance over his shoulder. The Jeep barreled on, devouring the distance between them.

Then, Leo saw something that sent a cold lance of shock through his body.

3
____

New York. Present Day.

"I've done alright with this, haven't I, girl?" Andy raised his bottled beer toward the apartment's floor-to-ceiling windows. The towers of Manhattan sparkled across the waters of the Hudson River.

"Yes, you have," Emma agreed, standing next to him and raising her glass too. Emma had never been to New York before and had to admit the view was beautiful. "Is that the —"

"Empire State Building, yeah." Andy pointed out the shining needle of the world-famous skyscraper. "I reckon this is the best view you'll get from anywhere in the city. When Michael said this place was available for the holidays, I just had to take it. How long has it been since we had a holiday?"

"At least since Frankie was born," Emma said, taking a sip of prosecco. She twirled the glass between her fingers. Emma and her friends used to drink bottles and bottles of the stuff a few years ago. Now she couldn't remember the last time she'd had even a single glass.

"Yeah, so well over two years." Andy tipped the remains of the beer into his mouth.

"Three years next month," Emma said absently.

Emma's gaze shifted from the city across the water to her husband. Although she had always wanted to visit New York, now that they were here, she didn't feel that excited. She clenched her hands, cursing herself. They were here on holiday, just the three of them. She should be excited.

"It's not just that brother of yours who gets to go on holiday. We can have them too." Andy grabbed another beer from the fridge.

"They go away for work, really —"

"You call that work." Andy laughed out loud. "That Leo wouldn't know a day's work if it punched him in the face. We need the holiday more than him. We deserve it." Andy sauntered across the room and draped an arm around his wife. "And it's supposed to snow in a few days. How magical will that be? New York in the snow. It'll be like a fairy tale."

Emma nodded but didn't say anything. Andy put the fresh bottle to his lips and guzzled down a third. Neither of them spoke for almost a minute. When Andy broke the silence, his tone was serious. "The last year's been pretty tough, hasn't it?"

Emma nodded. "It has been a challenge," she said, not bringing herself to drop her cheerful demeanor. "There's just been a lot of change for me... for us," Emma added, quickly. Whilst both their lives had changed dramatically since Frankie had come along, hers had changed unrecognizably.

"But I told you we could make it work, though, didn't I?" Andy physically puffed out his chest at the statement.

Emma opened her mouth to speak, but then realized she had no idea what to say. Instead, she just stared out at the skyscrapers and took another large swig. A boat slid regally up the river, its lights skipping across the water.

"You just needed to have a little faith in me, didn't you babes?" Andy continued, bravado now lacing his voice.

"I've always had faith in you," Emma said, trying not to sound bitter. "That's why I said yes when you asked me to marry you."

"It wasn't for my looks then?" Andy grinned.

"Well, there was that too," Emma said. She turned and eyed her husband. Back in those days, Andy's hours in the gym made him taut and muscular. Now his hours on the sofa and the beer he drank gave him a soft paunch and a hard temper.

Emma forced a smile. They were in New York, and they were going to have a great time reconnecting with each other. For once, it even sounded as if Frankie had gone straight to sleep.

Emma drained her glass, then smiled and kissed her husband.

"But I wanted to spend my life with you. That's why I said yes." She hugged Andy and looked at the city over his shoulder.

The strobing lights of a helicopter skipped between the towers. A night-time helicopter tour of Manhattan — now that's something she'd really love to do. There was no way they'd be able to afford to, though. Just to have a night out in the smoldering city would probably cost too much.

"It's a beautiful place, isn't it?" Andy said.

"Yes," Emma replied, forcing a smile. "It really is."

"What've we got for dinner, then?" Andy swigged the beer.

The pan on the stove rattled impatiently. Water hissed.

Gazing out at the skyline of the enchanting city, Emma had almost forgotten about dinner. She crossed to the kitchen and removed the lid from the pan.

"Pasta," Emma said. Steam billowed across the room.

"Nice." Andy sat at the table and rubbed his stomach. "As good as any Italian in this city, I reckon. You wouldn't come to New York for Italian food, anyway."

Emma's eyes flicked toward her husband. She didn't reply. Emma drained the pasta, stirred through the sauce, and separated it into two bowls.

"Get us another beer while you're up," Andy said.

Emma grabbed another bottle from the dwindling supply in the fridge, snapped it open, and gave it to Andy. Then she carried their dinner across to the table and sat down herself.

"Na babe, best pasta in New York," Andy said, slurping the first mouthful. "I can tell you that for sure."

Emma didn't hear him. She stared through the windows at the glinting city beyond.

"Open another bottle, babe. We're on holiday."

"I'm not sure I should. I mean, what if Frankie..."

"Nonsense. Let me... I'll do it for you." Andy hoisted himself up and lumbered across the open-plan living area. "We're on holiday. If my wife wants another glass of prosecco, then that's what she'll have."

"Okay, if you're sure." Emma smiled at Andy and looked longingly at the city beyond the window.

Andy cracked open the bottle and Prosecco gushed to the floor. "That's the way to do it. You need a bit to fizz up like that, otherwise you've not done it right. Here you go." He sloshed some into Emma's glass and thrust it in her direction.

"It's like that time we were staying… where was it we were staying? When we first met?" Andy said, slurping his sauce.

She took a sip of the prosecco, which had now simmered down to a third of the glass. "Manchester?".

"Yeah, that was it. That was a great weekend, wasn't it?"

"Yes, it was,"

Six months after they'd met, Andy had surprised Emma with a weekend away. It had been lovely but was the only example of such a gesture in their entire relationship.

"You know," Andy said, looking around, "we could have a place like this one day. If we wanted."

"Really? This would cost loads, wouldn't it?"

"Just a couple of million." Andy stifled a hiccup. "When my business takes off, we'll get something like this, no problem. We've had a good year so far and got some exciting contracts. I reckon things are going in the right direction."

Emma had seen the accounts. She knew that Andy's small-scale construction business was a fair way away from making a million in any currency.

"It's not all about the money, though." Emma turned to face her husband.

"Well, it sort of is, isn't it? It's money that got us here, and money pays for our house and food. I'd like to hear you say that if our accounts ran dry." Andy gulped his beer.

Emma thought of the well-paid job she'd given up when Frankie was born. *No son of mine will be sent away to some day-care place. A mum's job is to look after him,* had become a mantra of Andy's. It was an attitude which, despite all Emma's protests, her research into child development, and the financial benefits of keeping her salary, Andy just wouldn't drop. Emma had conceded in the end and spent the last three years almost single-handedly raising their son.

"Just you watch, babe," Andy grumbled. "I've got a few big contracts coming in, and they'll see us right."

The problem was, Andy had been saying that for years, leaving them struggling in the meantime.

Emma took a fortifying sip of the prosecco and sat up straight. They needed to have this conversation. She wasn't putting it off any longer.

∽

THE CITY WHISPERED and swished around him. To him, it seemed so obvious that he'd just killed someone. Yet, no one else had noticed. He had worried that the people he passed would sense it in his smile, see it in the flicker of his eyes, or the swing of his gait. But no, no one had noticed anything. To them, he clearly just looked like a normal guy. To him, everything was different.

A group of women passed him on the sidewalk, giggling beneath colorful umbrellas. He slowed and watched them, his head turning to follow. He stopped and for a long moment considered following the group.

"No, no, no," he muttered, shaking his head. "Not yet. Bide your time."

He continued, tracing the path he'd planned, tuning in to the quiet hum of the city. From the daytime chaos, the traffic had reduced to a few cars hissing through the puddles.

He gazed ahead and saw a taxi's bright headlights sparkling on the wet asphalt. On the other side of the street, a wisp of steam snaked from a drain in the frigid night air.

Then, the two-tone screech of sirens rose from the hubbub. The noise echoed fitfully from the surrounding buildings. The sirens neared. Blue and red lights flicked in nearby windows and a pair of police cruisers slid around the junction. Their tires shrieked across the road, as the drivers struggled to control their speed.

He turned away from the cars and examined the menu hanging in the window of a restaurant. He stepped to the side and peered through the glass. The place looked warm and inviting. It seemed to him, from the gloomy street and with the pressure of the blade in his sleeve, that the restaurant was another world entirely. A few diners glanced up as the police cars passed. The cars sped away and the diners returned to their civil conversation and expensive meals. To people like that, the sirens were like someone else's pain.

A large drip of rain caught him on the nose. He turned and continued traipsing through the deluge.

Although he'd achieved the first stage of his plan, the disturbance had frustrated him. He'd picked the place carefully for two reasons, one of which was its solitude. To complete all he desired, he only needed fifteen minutes undisturbed. That's all his great-grandfather had been allowed and look at what he'd achieved. Genius — that's what.

The events of the last few hours rode through his mind like a storm. Even though he hadn't gone all the way, the night had still been a success. He was now part of a small group of people, elevated high above most of humankind. He was a killer. He had taken someone's life with his own hands.

The grin now planted back on his face. He turned right at the intersection.

He hadn't been planning to kill again tonight. The night of the double murder wasn't for a while yet, but he'd only just begun to enjoy himself when his fun was curtailed.

The next site was close too, he knew, gripping the knife. And there was no time like the present.

4

"Gun!" Leo shouted, the word ripped away by the wind as soon as it left Leo's lips. Allissa needed no further explanation. She dipped forward over the bike, coaxing every ounce of speed from the engine.

Leo's gaze locked onto the jeep as a man leaned through the passenger's window. The man swung a rifle in their direction and fired. The spitfire rattle of automatic gunfire hammered through the air.

Instinctively, Allissa threw the bike into a desperate swerve. The rounds cracked wide, their trajectory carrying them into the forest.

"What's going on now?" Allissa asked, weaving them back into the center of the road.

Leo, his heart slamming against his ribs, scanned the road behind them again. Through the haze of dust and exhaust, he saw the passenger take aim again.

"Round two incoming!" Leo shouted, his voice almost lost in the wind. Allissa swung to the side again. Although the erratic path made them harder to hit, it also allowed the Jeep to close the distance.

"Don't worry," Allissa said, glancing over her shoulder, "I know a shortcut."

"I hate your shortcuts," Leo groaned, his teeth locked tightly together.

Allissa leaned and swung the bike sharply to the left, veering off the road onto a less-trodden jungle track. Branches whipped at their arms and legs, leaves fluttered in their wake.

The Jeep's tires screeched as the driver stamped on the brake. For a moment, it appeared the chase might end there. Then, with a guttural roar from the engine, the Jeep lurched back into motion, veering off the road and onto the narrow path.

The Jeep careened through the forest, bouncing over uneven terrain. Trees and shrubs cracked and snapped as the Jeep bulldozed its way through the undergrowth.

"No luck," Leo shouted, casting a furtive glance behind them. "They're still coming."

Allissa groaned and then hit the brake. The bike skidded, tires locking in a desperate bid to grip against the gravel. A harsh, grating sound filled the air.

"What are you doing?" Leo yelled.

As the bike fishtailed, he saw it — a small river loomed directly ahead.

Allissa angled the bike, her movements precise and deliberate, guiding them toward the river's edge. They hit the water, sending torrents splashing up all around them. The water churned and frothed as if trying to repel them back to land.

Allissa kept the throttle open, guiding them through the shallowest route from one bank to the other. Water erupted in towering curtains on either side, soaking them both. With a final surge, they cleared the river, skidding up the bank and back onto dry land.

Leo glanced over his shoulder. The Jeep burst from the undergrowth and powered straight into the water without so much as a pause. With its high chassis and four chunky tires, the driver didn't even need to slow to clear the shallow river.

Allissa wasted no time. She pulled back on the throttle and sent them slipping further down the narrow path. A hundred feet later, the bike burst out of the jungle and back onto the road.

With the winding path behind them, Allissa didn't let up. She swung the bike toward the nearest town, which involved navigating the sharply descending road.

Leo peered around Allissa as they approached the first in a series of switchback bends. A wonky sign with a faded arrow warned of the road's tight curves. Leo's breath hitched. Beyond the sign, he saw nothing but a perilous drop. There weren't even any guardrails, just open air, and the unforgiving sea hundreds of feet below.

Twenty seconds later, the Jeep roared out of the jungle path. The vehicle flew up the bank, leaving the ground for several feet and then slamming down on the tarmac. The tough suspension groaned but absorbed the shock with ease. Without missing a beat, the driver swung the wheel and gave chase.

Leo's grip on Allissa's waist tightened. His knuckles blanched and his fingers went numb. His stomach felt as though he were on a sinking ship in a storm. As they approached another bend, Allissa leaned into the turn, her body tense. Leo clamped his eyes closed, convinced that they were going to skid off the road completely.

The bike screamed around the corner. The tires slid

across the asphalt but somehow found grip. When they'd rounded the bend, Allissa straightened up and accelerated again.

Leo opened one eye, followed by the second. He peered to the side. Several hundred feet below them, the lights of the town twinkled against the dusk. Out across the Caribbean Sea, the sun was almost beneath the sea now, a path of gold shimmering in its wake.

A hail of gravel clattered as the jeep skidded around the corner behind them. The heavy vehicle leaned precariously, its tires squealing.

The jeep's headlights swung wildly, cutting through the twilight, and casting monstrous shadows that danced alongside them.

Allissa's hand clenched the brake as they careened toward the corner. The bike's frame leaned as they took the bend. Then, rounding the curve, the unexpected glare of headlights filled their vision. A minibus wound its way up the serpentine road. Bass-heavy music thumped from the minibus's beefed-up sound system.

Allissa threw her weight into the bike, coaxing it into a perilous lean, so close to the ground that Leo could swear he felt the asphalt grazing his shoes. The bike's tires spun on a knife edge.

The minibus blared its horn and swerved, missing Leo and Allissa by inches.

Allissa righted the bike, shooting past the now stationary minibus and heading for the town.

Leo glanced behind them to see the Jeep scream to a stop, the men already shouting at the minibus driver to get out of the way. Allissa accelerated, increasing their lead. For now, at least, they had got away.

5

—————

New York. Present Day.

"THERE'S something I want to talk to you about," Emma said, clasping the stem of the glass tightly between her hands. "Remember Danielle, the lady I used to work with?"

"Yeah," Andy grumbled angrily.

"Well, she's setting up a marketing agency, and she wants me to head up some accounts. She's been asking for a while, but last week she made me an offer. It's a fantastic offer."

Andy's mouth chewed over unsaid words. His eyes narrowed.

"How much?" he finally said.

The figure made Andy's face pale. It was almost three times what Andy's firm made in a year.

"I... I..." Andy fumbled the words, then got to his feet and paced across the kitchen. He did three laps of the room and then turned toward Emma, his face flushed red.

"I can't believe you've arranged this behind my back," Andy shouted across the room, his voice booming as though

Emma was hundreds of feet away. "How long have you been planning this?" Andy's eyes bored into Emma's. The muscles in his arms and shoulders stood rigid.

"I haven't arranged anything," Emma said calmly. "Danielle wants me to work there. She contacted me."

"I've told you to say no!" Andy bellowed.

"I said no at first," Emma said, raising her voice above his. "I did say no, but the more I think about it, the more it seems like a good idea. Andy, listen, it's a great offer. It's even too good to refuse."

A vein pulsed in Andy's forehead, looking as though it might burst.

"If I do this, then we could start paying off some debts and have regular holidays."

"What're we doing now?" Andy shouted, his arms flung wide. "This is a holiday, isn't it?"

Emma didn't reply.

"I'm providing you with holidays. Are you that selfish?" Andy's knuckles whitened around the bottle of beer. His tendons bulging like vines in the jungle, giving Emma the impression he might crack the bottle through frustration alone.

"Let me get this right." Andy's voice dropped to a malevolent whisper. "I'm out there, day and night, working my fingers to the bone to provide for this family. All the while, you're scheming of ways you think you can do it better?"

"No, it's not like that," Emma said, trying but struggling to remain calm. "It's not like that at all. I don't know why you're so against this. It's normal in a family for both parents to work. Plus, you didn't even let me finish. Danielle says I could work from home whenever I wanted. I could be totally flexible with my hours. We could both look after Frankie..."

"No way." Andy's fist crashed to the kitchen counter, startling Emma. The sound boomed through the apartment. "Look at this place." Andy swung his hand around the room as though he had constructed it personally. "This is what I've provided for you and Frankie. Look out there!" He marched across the room, pulled Emma forcefully up from the sofa, and turned her toward the window.

"This is what I provide for you, and you think you can do better?" Andy's fingers dug into Emma's skin. She winced at the pain.

"Let go. You're hurting me. Let go!"

Andy growled, removed his hands from Emma, and stormed over to the fridge. He downed the rest of his beer and grabbed another.

"I've been working day and night for this family," Andy reiterated, his words slurring. "You want to take that away from me, just like that?" He snapped his fingers.

"It's not about outdoing you," Emma said, anger boiling in her stomach now too. She pointed toward her husband. "I've tried to tell you this, but you won't listen. I want to go back to work, not just because of the money, but because I enjoy it and I'm good at it."

Andy's eyes almost completely closed. The muscles in his jaw tensed, bulging through his cheeks.

"You're good at being a mum," he said, his voice laced with menace. "And that's your job now."

Emma sighed. Her hands dropped to her sides and her whole body slumped.

"Yes, and I love being a mum," she said, almost sobbing. "But I need more conversation than listening to Frankie burble on all day."

Andy paced around the room again, mirroring the behavior of a caged animal.

"I know you've been working hard," Emma said. "I know that, but if I worked too, you wouldn't have to work quite so much. You could go out with your friends, go to the gym again, we could go on more holidays."

"We're here, aren't we?" Andy repeated, although with less conviction.

"We are," Emma whispered, "but we can't even afford to go out for a meal. It's hardly a holiday if we can't leave the apartment."

Something whizzed past Emma's vision in a blur. She felt the projectile sail just an inch past her. Hearing the beer bottle smash against the wall behind her, she realized what it was. She turned to face Andy, cowering with fear.

"That's what you want, isn't it?" Andy said. He wasn't shouting anymore. He was whispering, his tone dark and menacing. "You want to be out there living the high life, drinking cocktails and wearing posh clothes —"

"I'm not saying —"

"I know exactly what you're saying," he bellowed.

Andy stalked toward Emma. His fists, thick white balls.

"Alright, alright," Emma said, her hands outstretched in surrender. "Don't worry about it, we'll just..."

Andy took another step forward.

"Honestly, it's fine," Emma said, her eyes darting from the smashed bottle on the floor to her approaching husband. "I'll tell Danielle that family comes first, and I need to be there for you and Frankie."

Andy paused. His jaw clenched.

"Let me get you another drink. We'll enjoy the evening together." Emma scurried toward the kitchen. "I shouldn't have said anything. I'm sorry."

Andy grumbled something inaudible. His shoulders slumped.

"You've finished all the beers," Emma said, turning from the fridge. She opened Michael's spirit cupboard. "Sit down. I'll make you something from here. Forget I said anything, please."

Andy sunk into the sofa. Clearly still fuming with anger, his muscles remained tense.

Emma poured a generous measure of whiskey into a glass and returned to the couch.

"I know how hard you're working," she said again, sitting beside Andy. "I didn't mean to upset you. I'm sorry."

Andy accepted the glass and drank half of it straight away.

"It's just that I... I..." he mumbled. "I want you and Frankie to have... have the best things. You deserve that."

"And we do," Emma said.

Andy's thick hand slithered onto Emma's knee.

"You enjoy your drink, and I'll clean up this glass," Emma said. "I'd hate Frankie to see it or for it to stain."

Emma stood, and Andy's hand dropped to the leather. He gazed at his wife through unfocused eyes, then lifted the whiskey to his lips and downed it in one.

Emma stepped out of the front room and into the hallway. Now out of sight of her husband, she took a deep and panicked breath. She held the air for a few seconds and tried to calm her nerves. She glanced down at her hands, which were still shaking from the adrenaline, and then she caught sight of her pale reflection in the mirror.

At that moment, Emma thought about her life before Frankie was born. She had lots of friends and a busy social calendar. Now, she couldn't remember the last time she'd left the house. Andy met everything she suggested with scorn, saying it was either too expensive or not the sort of thing he wanted his wife and son to be doing. She was trapped.

Emma exhaled and took a long moment to calm herself, then wiped the moisture from her eyes. When she had begun to calm down, she fetched the dustpan and brush from the hallway closet and returned to the front room.

Andy lay on the sofa, his head tilted back, his mouth gaping, snoring loudly. His glass lay sideways on the floor.

A sign of relief escaped Emma's lips. At least this way she wouldn't have to talk to her husband again tonight.

"He gets like this," she said to herself apologetically. "Too much stress and too much beer. He'll be fine in the morning." She knelt and swept the broken glass in the dustpan.

Climbing back to her feet, Emma caught sight of Manhattan's skyline glimmering across the river.

There was a world of opportunity, out there, she thought. It was a world of opportunity that she was missing out on because of him. Feeling exhausted, Emma padded through to the bedroom and climbed between the sheets.

CHILDREN FEAR THE SHADOWS. He remembered being a child and fearing the shadows himself. Or rather, being a child and fearing what might lurk unseen in those shadows.

Adults weren't afraid. They'd checked enough shadows for goblins or monsters that now they just assumed there was nothing there. They didn't even bother to look anymore.

He smiled. It was funny, he thought as he nestled in the shadowy passage beside Hanbury's clothes shop. He had chosen Hanbury's on purpose. Expensive clothes shone beneath bright lights in the shop's window, right next to the place which would, with a bit of luck, be the scene of his second victim's demise.

He glanced down at the dark fabric of his raincoat. Here in the shadows, he was almost invisible. It looked as though he wasn't there at all. He was like an exterminating angel, manifesting from the darkness and bringing death to his chosen one.

He narrowed his eyes against the intensifying rain. It would have been like this in London all those years ago.

"This is the best way to do it," he muttered, glancing around at the dark passageway again. This was the perfect scene for his performance. This was his theater. It amused him that he sounded like an expert now. Of course, he was an expert. He was a killer.

Choosing a victim this way was best because, on the face of it, he had no reason to kill these women. If you thought about it logically, as people often did, he didn't even know them. There was no link whatsoever between him and these people — other than they happened to be in the same place at the same time. He'd watched enough documentaries and read enough true crime stories to know that suspicion automatically fell on the victim's friends. Everyone's closet was full of skeletons, and some skeletons were worth killing for.

His motivations were different, though. The victims themselves weren't important. They were like an artist's paint or a sculptor's marble. They were a means to an end. It was, of course, the end that would make it all worthwhile.

A car passed, its tires hissing through the rain. He ducked further into the shadow to avoid the glare. The brake lights flickered on, bathing the street in a violent red. The car screeched to a stop, and the door clunked open.

"Thanks for nothing," came an aggressive female voice.

"I told you to stop three times back there. You should have been paying attention..."

He couldn't hear the driver's response.

"No, forget it. I'm not paying you to go around again. Next time just listen, alright?"

His fingers closed around the knife.

"You can absolutely forget about the tip. I want that change."

The taxi sloshed away. This was it.

6

———

St Lucia. Present Day.

As the evening beckoned, the locals set about transforming the town center from a market to the setting for their weekly street party. A truck piled high with speakers was inched into position and strings of bulbs flickered to life. Market stalls were re-purposed, now stocked with beer, rum, or the ubiquitous fried chicken, the spicy scent of which tingled nostrils for hundreds of feet in all directions.

Allissa pulled the bike to a stop at the edge of the main street and assessed the scene. Several hundred people crammed the streets, and the air thrummed with the pulsating rhythms of Caribbean music. She cut the bike's engine and the vibrant soundtrack of laughter, the sizzle of street food hitting the grill, joined in the melee.

"What are you doing?" Leo said. "We need to get out of here!"

"How do you suggest we do that?" Allissa pointed at the mixed crowd of locals and tourists who had turned up for the weekly celebration. "Even if we managed to get the bike through the crowd, everyone would see us. There will be several thousand witnesses to say where we've gone. Right now, we can blend in and then sneak away."

Leo nodded reluctantly and shuffled off the seat. As his feet touched the ground, his legs wobbled beneath him as the vibrations of the chase continued to buzz through his muscles.

Allissa slid the bike in beside two others and kicked down the stand. She glanced at the vehicle; the paintwork was now scratched, and filth covered the tank and seat.

"I don't think we'll get our deposit back from the rental company," Allissa said, pointing at the bike. Leo couldn't quite tell in the gloom, but it looked as though Allissa was grinning.

"Wait a second," Leo said, pointing at his friend. "You enjoyed that?"

"It was great, wasn't it? Did you see how we took that corner up there..."

"And nearly killed us. I still can't feel my feet!" Leo swung the bag, which contained the surveillance equipment, onto his back and took a shaky step forward.

"Oh, come on, it wasn't that bad." Allissa put her arm through Leo's and pulled them toward the crowd. "But we really should get a move on. This crowd is the perfect cover."

Suddenly, the sound of a revving engine cut through the deep bassline. Leo whipped around just in time to see a motorbike speed around the corner. Registering that the sound didn't come from the Jeep, he visibly relaxed.

Allissa led them further into the crowd, winding between a group of local women with long colorful braids and a pair of suntanned tourists. Leo took a deep breath, attempting to calm his nerves, and almost coughed on the smell of jerk chicken and fried plantains. They took another few steps further forward and were swallowed by a sea of people, hips cloaked in vibrant reds, yellows, and greens. The DJ, positioned high above the crowd on the back of the truck, mixed seamlessly into the next tune and the crowd roared in appreciation.

"Rum punch, you wan' rum punch?" A woman shouted from behind one of the stalls, which had now become a makeshift bar, illuminated by a string of lights.

Allissa pulled them over toward the stall. "We'll take two," she said, shouting over the noise.

"What? No!" Leo said, his body jolting upright. "We need to get out of here. We are in mortal danger here. This is no time to chill out and drink rum."

"Yeah, I know what you're going to say," Allissa said, leaning in close to Leo's ear. "Those men might turn up and..."

"Exactly that," Leo said, folding his arms tightly across his chest.

"But you know what those dangerous men will be looking for?" Allissa said.

"Yeah! Me and you! They saw us on the bike!" Leo pointed in the direction from which they'd come.

"Those men will be looking for two terrified looking people trying to get away. The best thing for us to do is to blend in."

Allissa bent over the stall and said something to the seller. The woman smiled, nodded, and then trotted up the stairs and into one of the buildings. At the top of the stairs, she turned and beckoned Leo and Allissa inside.

"What are we doing?" Leo said, his eyes panning the street in shock.

"Follow me and you'll find out." Allissa scampered up the stairs and into the building, which clearly served as a shop during the day.

The woman disappeared into the back room, reemerging thirty seconds later with several brightly colored garments.

"It might be a bit on the tight side for you, but I think it'll do jus' fine," the saleswoman said, passing Allissa a brightly colored, flowy dress printed with bold patterns.

"Where you from?" The woman said, shouting over the music.

"We're from England," Allissa replied, heading to the changing room to slip into the dress.

She emerged a moment later wearing the dress.

"I been to Englan'," the shopkeeper yelled in reply.

Allissa spun around the room.

Three women wandered in, cheering, and clapping to a song they clearly loved.

"Naaa, England's a cool place," the shopkeeper said. "When I say cool, I mean cold! Brrrrr!" She animated a shiver. "I remember getting off the plane when I first arrived in Englan', I went for a smoke outside the airport. I pulled on the cigarette proper deep. Hadn't had one in hours. Then, when I breathed out, the smoke just didn't stop! I was like, how big are these lungs?"

The tune changed, and the crowd outside erupted into whoops and cheers.

Leo's gaze was involuntarily drawn to Allissa's body. Up until they'd finally found Leo's long-lost ex-girlfriend a few weeks ago, Allissa had been an ally and friend. But now, different and potentially dangerous feelings loomed within him.

Allissa spun around again, and the light played tricks with the fabric, which clung to her like a second skin. Allissa pulled her hair out from the band under which she'd kept it all day and arranged some flowers in it.

The saleswoman passed Leo a shirt which boasted a patchwork of vivid colors and then a pair of lime green trousers. Knowing his life, literally, depended on it, Leo changed without a fuss. The saleswoman then draped garlands of flowers around them both.

Leo glanced at their reflections in a full-length mirror and had to admit that the change was nothing short of miraculous. Allissa handed a bundle of notes to the woman as Leo stuffed their old clothes into the bag along with the camera.

Outside the shop, Leo once again scanned the street just in time to see the Jeep speed toward the crowd and brake aggressively. The Jeep idled for several seconds a few feet away from the dancers, its horn beeping and lights flashing. The partygoers, involved in the music, didn't even notice.

The revelers, lost in the intoxicating embrace of the music, continued to dance to the beat.

Clearly frustrated that they'd lost their quarry, two imposing figures climbed from the Jeep. From his vantage point, Leo got a look at the brutes. Their bodies were thick set. He suspected those muscles were not homed in gyms but in the brutal business of their trade. The men moved with a predatory grace, scanning the crowd with intent.

The thugs stepped toward the crowd, tucking handguns beneath their stained vests.

They shoved through the crowd, broad shoulders parting the sea of bodies with ease.

"Don't even look at them," Allissa hissed through a fake smile. "We're here enjoying the party, remember?"

"I just hope this works," Leo said, painting a smile on his face and following Allissa back down to the street. Allissa pulled them into the crowd, her hips already moving effortlessly to the pounding beat.

"Stop!" a voice bellowed across the crowd.

A chill shot up Leo's spine. Every muscle fiber in his body coiled tight. He whipped around and his eyes fell upon the vendor holding out two cups of rum punch.

"It's not a party if you don't have one of these," the woman said, her smile as broad as it had always been.

"Sure, thanks," Leo said, accepting the cups and passing one to Allissa. He took a fortifying sip. The liquid was cool and sweet with a fiery kick.

As the crowd pulsed to the vibrant fusion of soca and reggae, Leo and Allissa wound their way through. Allissa moved with a natural fluidity, her body finding the heartbeat of the music with ease. She danced as if born to it, each step and sway an echo of the rhythm. She rolled her hips in time with the bass and lifted her arms in graceful arcs.

A few feet behind, Leo tried to copy Allissa's natural grace but found his body moving stiffly. He tried to match the rhythm of the music, but always felt as though he were a beat behind.

Leo spun around, attempting to disguise the fact he was scanning the crowd as some kind of strange dance move. He saw the thugs pushing their way through the crowd fifty feet away. Leo froze, and his feet shuffled to a stop. Although the pair were still some distance away, Leo felt the desire to run stiffen his muscles.

Leo stood motionless for several seconds — a solitary stationary figure in a sea of movement.

"You need to look as though you're enjoying yourself," Allissa snapped, jabbing him in the ribs. "If you're going to stand there like a soldier on duty, you'll give the game away. Just do this." Allissa took Leo's hands and placed them on her hips. Allissa spun around, leading Leo through the dancing people.

Anxiety warred with attraction as Allissa's body gyrated beneath the dress. Leo felt the now familiar bolt of energy move through him when they got close.

"Fine," Leo said, allowing himself to be led through the crowd. "But we need to get out of here. We should double back the way we came."

Allissa spun around several times and steered them through the throng, their movements now part of the dance.

Leo glanced at the thugs as they drew level. The men were walking side by side, less than twenty feet away. Taller than most of the dancers, the thugs scanned the crowd, checking each person for their quarry.

Leo's anxiety reached fever pitch as Allissa pulled them closer still. She held her hands high, embodying the carnival dancer, and spun Leo around, facing away from the men. Drawing level with the thugs, Allissa pulled Leo in close, and the pair twisted again, ducking out of sight. They scurried several feet, bent below the heads of the other dancers. Now out of their pursuers' eyeline, they wove through clusters of dancers.

At the end of the street, Leo turned and peered back. The thugs continued to push their way in the opposite direction, checking each of the dancers in turn.

"There look," Allissa said, pointing at a minibus idling at the end of the road. "I don't care where it's going. Let's get on."

Leo and Allissa darted toward the bus and slipped on

board just as the doors closed. The vehicle was almost full of people heading home after the party. Allissa led them to the front and sat beside the driver.

The vehicle lurched forward, the world outside the windows blurring into streaks of color. As the bus rattled away from the party, Leo and Allissa peered through the window at the now abandoned Jeep.

7

Andy opened his eyes slowly. "Emma?" He blinked and rubbed a hand across his face.

The apartment was dark. "What the..."

He remembered the conversation with Emma which had led into the row about her returning to work. Then he recalled the hazy, drink-fueled rage that had consumed his mind before everything went black.

He slurred a series of swear words.

Andy struggled to his feet, the room spinning around him. He rolled his shoulders and then winced. His back and neck ached. He rubbed a hand across his shoulders, but it didn't seem to help. He staggered across to the kitchen counter and held on to the marble top. After a few seconds, the spinning room slowed down ever so slightly.

Andy did a three-sixty but saw no sign of Emma in the living area. Emma must have gone to bed without him. Andy muttered to himself. Deep in his gut, he had the distinct feeling that he'd done something terrible. He examined the room once again, with more attention this time, but couldn't see any evidence of his misdeeds. There weren't even any empty glasses in the kitchen. The city shone through the window.

"Can't blame a working man for having a few drinks on holiday," Andy moaned, attempting to appease the fear, which was now getting uncomfortable.

He padded through to the bedroom and snapped on the light. Emma lay in the bed, breathing lightly.

"Hey Em, I'm sorry," he said. "I shouldn't have —"

Emma didn't reply, still sleeping soundly.

"Emma?" Andy muttered, frowning. "Come on, this is all a bit over the top, isn't it?" He shook her gently, but she continued to snooze. "This is a bit over the top. Let's just talk about this. Couples fight all the time."

Andy shook Emma again but got no reply.

"If you want to be like that, fine." He huffed, turned around, and stomped back into the living room. He paced around the living room, his original anger returning with vengeance.

"I can't believe you've done this," Andy growled. "I arranged this holiday. It was all my idea. You don't get to go off and have a better time on your own."

Andy's eyes fixed on the bottle of whiskey still sitting on the kitchen counter. A pang of recognition chimed somewhere. He assumed he must have been drinking this too. He crossed the room, snagged up the bottle, and examined the logo.

"Looks expensive," he muttered, twisting off the top and taking a sip. "Tastes it too." That was the thing about Michael, Andy thought, he had good taste.

Andy took another swig of the whiskey and considered how unfair it all was. Michael's wife, Maria, stayed at home to be a mum. Why did Emma make such a fuss over it? It wasn't like he was asking something outrageous of her. He just wanted her to stay at home and look after their son. Her son!

Andy quelled his anger with another swig of the whiskey and stepped across to the window. New York's skyline flickered across the river.

Andy's rage spiked again. He patted down his pockets and then realized he didn't have any money.

"I bet Michael will have some," Andy muttered. He strode across to the kitchen and rummaged through the drawers and cupboards. He shoved cutlery, crockery, and saucepans aside, but found nothing.

He paused his search to have another drink and then stalked over to a side table. He pulled the draws out one by one and rummaged through. His face contorted into a grin. Inside, amongst a load of papers, was a gold watch, a few rings, a crisp bundle of notes, and a set of car keys.

"I knew you'd come through for me, Michael," Andy whispered.

He slid the notes into his pocket and examined the watch. It looked expensive. Andy then picked up the car keys.

"Yes, the Porsche," Andy said, examining the keys. Seeing a picture of Michael's Porsche online a few months ago had made Andy resent his seven-year-old Honda Civic. Andy glanced at the keys in his sweaty palm and smirked.

He turned and looked at himself in the mirror. Without another thought, he shoved open the apartment door and called the elevator.

The lights in the underground car park snapped on as Andy staggered out of the elevator. He thumbed the key and the lights of a red Porsche Boxster flashed.

Andy slid into the driver's seat and put the bottle in the central console beside him. He pressed the start button. The

Porsche grumbled to life. The twin exhausts thundered through the car park. He pumped the accelerator, and the grumble became an all-out roar. Andy poked at the screen on the dash. Eventually, he figured out how to program the satellite navigation system for a journey into Manhattan. The directions filled the screen. Andy pulled on his seatbelt and took another swig of the whiskey. Then, snapping the car into drive, he slid the Porsche out of the car park.

"New York, are you ready?" Andy whooped, pulling out onto Hoboken's wide streets. It was late, and the night was quiet. He stopped at a traffic light. The Porsche's engine grumbled, begging for speed.

A pair of women walked along the street, probably on their way home from a bar. Andy lowered the window and smiled. The lights changed, and he floored the accelerator. The Porsche flew ahead. Andy pushed the car harder. His teeth bared with exhilaration.

He followed the sat nav's directions and turned right onto the turnpike for the Lincoln Tunnel. Manhattan's skyline flashed across the river.

"New York, baby!" he shouted through the car's open window.

Andy swung the Porsche toward the Lincoln Tunnel, leaving a set of tire marks on the road behind him. He approached the barrier and padded the brake pedal. The barrier popped up and the yawning mouth of the tunnel beckoned him on. He didn't need any further encouragement and floored the gas.

The Porsche's engine groaned as the revs climbed to a frenetic crescendo. The tachometer's needle danced far beyond the red line. The car roared into the tunnel, the sound of the engine reverberating from the concrete walls.

Through bloodshot eyes, Andy watched the car devour

the asphalt. The row of lights on the roof of the tunnel strobed hypnotically across the windshield. Andy adjusted the wheel and took the car into the outside lane, screaming past a lumbering bus.

He glanced down and saw the speedometer climbing further. It felt as though the Porsche was begging for speed — a request Andy was happy to oblige.

The tunnel stretched before him, its walls blurring as they funneled him into the impending bend. Oblivious to the danger, Andy increased the pressure on the gas pedal.

Warning signs flickered past in the blink of an eye, not even registering in Andy's intoxicated vision.

The noise of the engine filled the space with a primal growl, rebounding like gunfire within the confines of the tunnel. The needles pushed higher. Lights on the dash strobed red, warning the driver that the vehicle was approaching its limits.

Andy touched the brake, sending a shudder through the chassis. The brakes let out a piercing cry, and the tires left thick rubber streaks on the roadway.

The Porsche skated perilously across the lanes, no longer under human control. Fortunately, at this time of night, the tunnel was deserted.

Andy's hands gripped the wheel, which still felt as light as a feather. He narrowed his eyes, focusing as hard as his intoxicated mind would allow. He fixed his gaze on the tunnel's vanishing point, curving ahead. Bracing himself, not knowing whether the action would bring the Porsche back under his control, or send it into a violent tailspin, Andy applied the brake again. Tires squealed, and the vehicle lurched like a beast trying to break free. The next few seconds passed like hours, and eventually, it felt like the car was coming back under his control. He coaxed the brake, pulling the speedometer down into the two-figures range.

Then Andy saw something that sent ice into his veins. His intoxication evaporated in a heartbeat, and Andy felt as though he could see in perfect clarity. He tried to glance away, looking for a solution, but couldn't. Now that Andy had seen the threat, his eyes remained locked.

A large maintenance truck, surrounded by flashing lights and cones, crept along in the center of the tunnel. Andy's eyes widened. His body jarred into position.

The Porsche lurched toward the truck, taking out a line of traffic cones. The cones thumped up across the windshield and skittered around the car. One hit the glass, bouncing away with a dull thump.

Now acting on instinct, a last-ditch attempt to save his life, Andy hit the brake. Each of his muscles taut he twisted the wheel, trying to manhandle the Porsche into the other lane.

The car slowed, but not enough. The cat's eyes in the center of the roadway pulsated through the car, shaking his tensed shoulders.

The Porsche roared on, hurtling toward the truck's looming bulk.

Lights streaked overhead, the car moving at such a speed that they looked like one single bulb.

Gritting his teeth, Andy watched the late-night road workers running for their lives. They shouted warnings to one another, their shouts swallowed by the roar of the Porsche's engine and the thump of the scattering cones.

Andy's heart hammered against his ribs. His decision was a stark one; keep straight ahead for the unforgiving back of the truck; swing to the side for the unyielding curve of the tunnel's concrete wall. With a desperate twist, Andy wrenched the wheel, his muscles tensing, his breath a sharp intake.

For an instant, nothing happened. Then the Porsche obeyed, lurching violently to the right. The world became a blur, the tunnel spinning like a vortex.

Time dilated, stretching the moment of impact into a series of slow-moving images. Metal kissed the concrete with a sickening crunch, a symphony of destruction booming for hundreds of feet in both directions. The airbag exploded, blocking Andy's view. The car spun, its chassis rolling over with the grace of a wounded animal. Glass rained like diamonds. Fuel and other liquids sloshed out in all directions.

Andy was thrown like a rag doll against the inflated airbag, then the seat, then back again. He closed his eyes, not knowing which way was which.

The screech of tearing metal hammered through the tunnel. The vehicle landed on its roof and continued sliding down the roadway.

Darkness fell over Andy like an unwelcome dusk, followed by silence.

8

EMMA WOKE up to the sound of an electronic buzz hammering through the apartment. She blinked a few times as she tried to work out where she was. The room around her was dark, but something about it seemed unfamiliar. She rolled over and clicked on a bedside lamp, which she was sure she'd never seen before. A digital clock on the nightstand told her it was still early in the morning.

The jarring noise echoed through the apartment again.

Emma sat up and the memories came back to her bit by bit. First, she realized they were staying at Andy's brother's house, then she remembered the argument. She rubbed her eyes and climbed to her feet. The room spun around her for a few seconds. She noticed the jar of sleeping pills on the bedside table and remembered the recommendation to take one to help with the jet lag. She clearly hadn't counted on the few glasses of wine she'd consumed too.

The noise came again. Even though it was an emotionless, electronic buzz, to Emma it sounded jarring and urgent.

She rushed out into the hallway and followed the noise to the intercom system.

She picked up the entry system's receiver, and the small screen flickered to life.

"It's the Hoboken Police Department." An urgent voice came down the line. "You're going to have to let us in."

Nausea welled in Emma's stomach as she opened the apartment door. A churning, bubbling, acidic torrent rose in her throat. She leaned against the wall and tried to control it.

The elevator doors slid open, and two police officers stepped out. One was a stocky man with tightly curled hair, the other an Asian woman.

"Good morning." The female officer spoke first. "We're looking for a Michael Harris. Is he here?"

Emma's mouth opened, but no words came out. Her sense of sickness soared.

"Come in, come in." Emma beckoned desperately. "Michael's not here, no. He's my brother-in-law. My husband and I are house-sitting for him." Emma looked anxiously from one officer to the other, tension knotting her chest.

"How long have they been away, Mrs...?"

"Emma, please. They went three days ago, and we arrived yesterday."

"Have either of you used his car during the time you've been here?" The male officer glanced at a notepad. "A red Porsche Boxster."

"No, we haven't. We only arrived yesterday afternoon and haven't been out since. Why?"

"Mr. Harris's car was involved in an incident last night. We're trying to understand what happened."

"What?" Emma gasped. "That's not possible. It must

have been stolen or something. Did anyone see the person driving it?"

"No, the car was empty by the time we arrived."

Emma shook her head and looked from the police officers to a spot on the floor where the fragments of the bottle had been. "It must have been stolen or something. We've not used it." She looked up. "I didn't even know Michael had a car."

"Are we able to speak with your husband, too? Just to see if he noticed anything," the male officer interjected.

"Of course," Emma said. "I'll go wake him. We had a long flight yesterday. I went to bed before him, and he must have slept in the other room so as not to disturb me."

Emma turned and walked toward the other bedroom. She crossed the hall and pushed open the bedroom door. Then she gasped and fell against the wall for support.

"Mrs. Harris, are you okay?" The police officers rushed after her. Emma didn't hear. The officers appeared at Emma's side.

"Is this the bedroom Mr. Harris was supposed to be staying in?"

"I think so." Emma nodded.

"I'll check the other rooms," the female officer said, heading for the hallway. She appeared back at the door a few seconds later. "Nothing. The apartment's empty." The officer led Emma from the scene of destruction into the living room. Emma sunk into the cushions, her eyes bleary.

"What we're dealing with here is a missing person," the woman said.

The male officer spoke quietly into his radio.

"Mrs. Harris," — the female officer crouched in front of Emma — "we will find your husband. I'm going to ask you a few questions now."

THE KILLER STOOD up and looked down at the body. Her neck was twisted at a strange angle. One arm extended upwards, the other bent beneath her.

He gripped the knife in his right hand. A trickle of blood dripped from the tip and puddled on the concrete.

He couldn't help but feel disappointed. Knife slashes crisscrossed her face, and he'd stabbed her three times in the stomach. She would never look as radiant as his first. In his mind's eye, he pictured the pearly-white skin of his first victim lying in the gloom.

He was angry that this one was already disfigured. He hadn't wanted her to look this way, but she was now ruined because she couldn't die as he needed her to.

"Why did you have to fight back?" he murmured. "It would have been so much better if you hadn't fought back."

He wondered whether he'd got lucky with the first one. He certainly felt like there was something special about her. He remembered her life ebbing peacefully away with every pump of blood. That was the feeling he'd craved. It was heavenly. He'd watched her eyes flutter for the last time as she slid from this life and into the next.

The result was the same, though; he supposed — a crumpled body in an alleyway. Although this one looked far from heavenly. There wasn't time to complain. There wouldn't be time for anything. He needed to get to work.

He bent over and cut open her bright yellow coat. He wanted to get that out of sight, should anyone notice it from the street. He pulled the coat out from beneath her and threw it behind a dumpster.

He straightened her arms. She looked better with her arms at her sides.

He cut off her blood-soaked jumper and threw that behind the dumpster too. Her stomach was punctuated by three ferocious stab wounds. He hadn't planned to stab her, but he'd needed to stop the shrieking.

"Why did you have to make all that noise?" he asked, as though she might actually answer him. He snarled and tightened his grip on the knife.

It didn't really matter though, he thought. He wouldn't let it matter. She's made the ultimate sacrifice for him — that's all that mattered.

He pulled up the left sleeve of his raincoat and looked at the bracelet. It wasn't what she looked like to start with — that wasn't the point — it was what he did with her that was going to make the difference. He lifted the bracelet to his lips and kissed it.

"This is for you," he whispered. "It's all in honor of you."

9

———

"THAT WAS CLOSE," Allissa said as they walked from the bus stop and through the grounds of the hotel in which they'd been staying for the last few nights. Insects hummed and zinged from the bushes. Lights reflected across the surface of the pool like a bed of jewels. Wind hissed through the palm trees, and the sea purred against the sand.

"It looks like we've got the place to ourselves," Leo said, tasting the sticky sweetness of the rum punch on his tongue.

"This way," Allissa said, leading them down to the beach. "Midnight swimming!" She broke into a run toward the waves.

"No way!" Leo shouted as loud as he dared. "That's dangerous. Don't go in there!"

Allissa rounded a pair of palm trees and disappeared into the gloom. Leo gave chase and then froze. He squinted toward the sea but couldn't see Allissa against the great mass of night. His heart pounded, and his breathing quickened. He waited a few seconds for his eyes to adjust to the lack of light, but still couldn't see any further than a few feet in front of him.

"Don't go in there," Leo bellowed toward the sea. He paced across the sand. "I don't want to have to come in and drag you out!"

"Oh, come on," she said, appearing by his side. "What sort of reckless idiot do you think I am?" Laughing, Allissa dropped to the sand and stretched out her legs. "This is a beautiful place, though."

Leo sat beside her, and they both gazed out at the moon hanging low and ripe above the water, its tail shimmering.

"It's beautiful. Yet again, I'm sorry that our trip ended up running away from gun-wielding mad men."

Allissa shrugged. "I'm used to it now. I think I've just accepted that every time we leave the house, gun-wielding madmen are a distinct possibility," Allissa said, mocking Leo's voice.

"What? It's true. Whatever we do, people end up coming after us." Leo turned toward her, his tone much more serious.

"Oh, I agree," Allissa said, suppressing a giggle. "I just find the dramatic way you describe it constantly amusing."

"Look, I don't mind this life on the run sometimes," Leo said, trying to sound serious, "but once in a while, it would just be nice to go somewhere without a group of merciless killers in hot pursuit."

"Merciless killers in hot pursuit!" Allissa said, now howling with laughter. "You should write these down for a thriller novel."

They both laughed for almost two minutes, the tension of the evening coming out in great giggles and snorts. When the laughing subsided, Leo lay back on the sand and let the wrestling ocean and the distant mumble of the jungle fill his senses. Many years ago, in therapy for his anxiety, Leo had started the practice of concentrating on the surrounding sounds. It was a habit that had stuck, and now, Leo listened closely to it all.

"Remember that afternoon in Kathmandu, when you turned up at the guesthouse pretending to be my brother?" Allissa said, tracing a line in the sand with her finger. The silver moonlight bathed the beach, giving her skin an ethereal glow.

"Of course," Leo replied, glancing up at her. "I don't think I'll ever forget that."

"Did you ever think it would end up like this? Even for a moment." Allissa looked down at Leo, lying on his back.

"Not in a million years. Absolutely no way. It's like a film." Leo propped himself up on his elbows, his fingers toying awkwardly with the fallen frond of a palm tree.

"It has been a bit like a film," Allissa said, leaning toward him too. "A dangerous film full of merciless murdering madmen."

"That's a good one!" Leo said, "Maybe you've got a knack for this dramatic language thing, too. But yes, it has been dangerous, that's true."

"If it were a film, who do you think would play you?" Allissa asked.

"Now that is a tough one because he'd have to be super attractive, intelligent, and physically at the top of his game."

Allissa roared with laughter and then poked Leo in the stomach. "With a washboard stomach formed by weeks of hotel food?"

"That's right!" Leo said, too. He pulled Allissa's hands out from behind her, and she fell to the sand beside him. The pair laughed for a minute, and then Allissa turned to face Leo. Their faces were now just a few inches apart.

"It's been strange," Allissa said after a few seconds of silence had passed. "I don't think I've ever spent as much time with anyone as I have over the last few months with you. After all those years of traveling on my own... running away on my own, I suppose I should call it. I just thought I was the sort of person who did stuff alone." Allissa became silent for a moment.

Leo swept his fingers through the sand.

"This has kinda crept up on me, I think. That's why, if you'd told me a year ago that things would end up here, on this beach, you and me, I just wouldn't have believed it. Am I talking rubbish, or does that make sense?"

"It makes total sense to me," Leo said, shuffling forward a fraction of an inch. There was so much he wanted to say but was also lost in the sound of Allissa's voice. He didn't want her to stop.

"I was just so used to being independent. I thought I liked it that way, and don't get me wrong, I did. I think that in the past I wasn't spending the time with the right people, that was the problem." Allissa looked at the inky black ocean across Leo's shoulder for a few moments. "Do you think we'll still be doing stuff like this next year?"

Without another word Leo shuffled forward again, his lips heading toward Allissa's. He took a deep breath and reveled in the coconut scent of her hair mixing with the sand and sea. This was a moment he knew he'd want to remember.

A sound jarred between them. To start with, it was only faint, like the distant call of some night creature. Then it came again, louder this time.

Leo jerked backward, the romance of the situation suddenly ebbing away. The noise came again. This time, he recognized it as the electronic buzzing of his phone.

"Are you going to get that?" Allissa said, shaking her head gently.

"Absolutely not," Leo said, "There's no one I want to talk to that isn't here right now."

The phone buzzed from within Leo's pocket another few times and then fell silent.

They locked eyes, close in the darkness. Without a word, Leo once again shuffled toward Allissa. Then, right at that moment, his phone buzzed again.

"Someone really wants to speak to you," Allissa said, once again straightening up.

Leo reluctantly shuffled the phone from his pocket and glanced at the screen.

"It's Emma," Leo said, paling with worry. Reading her name on the screen, his stomach tightened. There was no way she would be calling if it wasn't important. "Hi, Emma, are you okay?" Leo answered the call and held the phone to his ear.

The sound Emma made told Leo that everything was far from okay.

"It's... it's Andy," Emma said, her voice barely intelligible between sobs. "Last night. We had an argument, and now he's gone."

"Hold on," Leo said, stopping his sister before she got fully into the explanation. He covered the phone and locked eyes with Allissa. Leo's expression made it crystal clear that something wasn't right. The pair jumped to their feet and ran up to Leo's room.

"We're going to sort this. We're going to find him," Leo said two minutes later, both sitting on the bed. A bumping noise came down the line, and then Emma sobbed. Leo passed Allissa his laptop so that she could take notes on the call.

"Allissa is here now, taking notes," Leo said.

"Hi Emma," Allissa said, instantly sympathetic. "As Leo

says, just tell us in your own words. I'll stop you if I need anything repeated. It's crucial that we know everything."

Emma sniffed her agreement and explained the events of the previous night, culminating in the visit from the police.

"What's the address of Andy's brother's place?" Allissa asked.

Leo felt a pang of guilt that he didn't even know Andy's brother lived in New York. He probably had been told that piece of information but given that he didn't like Andy, had filed it in the recesses of his memory.

Emma gave the address.

"Is Frankie okay?" Allissa asked.

"Yes, he's having a nap at the moment," Emma's voice warmed momentarily at the mention of her son. "I don't think he's even realized that his daddy's not here."

"Let's go back to last night," Allissa said. "You had an argument. Is that unusual?"

Leo privately suspected that arguments with Andy were more common than Emma would like to admit.

Emma talked them through the argument, describing how things had escalated after she'd told him about the job offer.

"Has Andy ever been violent toward you?" Allissa asked.

Leo winced at the question. He looked down at the phone, waiting for Emma's response.

For a long moment, the line was silent.

"No," Emma said, finally. "A couple of times I thought he was about to be. I even braced myself for it, but he's never actually done it."

Allissa made a note of that.

"What mood was he in when you left last night?" Leo asked.

"He was angry. It was a stupid argument, really. I shouldn't have wound him up. It's my fault. I know what he gets like."

"No, it's not your fault," Allissa interjected. "This is all on him. None of this is your fault."

"How long are you staying there?" Leo asked, taking the conversation to more comfortable ground.

"Two weeks. We're spending Christmas here. Andy's brother is with his wife's family in Florida."

Leo and Allissa's eyes met. Leo spoke first. "How soon can we get to New York?"

10

LEO JUDDERED with anxiety as the plane's nose dipped and they descended toward New York.

Lost in the hazy half-sleep he could only ever manage on flights, the change in direction caused his mind to jump into a panic. His eyes shot open, expecting a scene of chaos as they plummeted toward the ocean below.

Of course, everything was normal and serene as it should be. Leo took a deep breath and stretched as best he could in the confines of the seat. Allissa slept beside him. She snored lightly with her head tilted to the side. Leo let the breath go, and his anxiety faded.

Everything was fine.

Leo had suffered from anxiety for years. It came sporadically, with no logic or reason. Sometimes weeks would pass without an attack. Other times, two in the same day would tear through his consciousness.

He gazed out the window and thought about the investigation that would start as soon as they landed.

"Are we nearly there?" Allissa mumbled, stirring from her sleep. She pulled out her earbuds and glanced at Leo.

"Yeah, coming in to land soon," Leo said, scrutinizing the buildings below.

The action film Leo had attempted to watch before dozing reached its climax on the screen in front of him. A band of superheroes appeared to be winning against the villains. It was a simple fight, good versus evil, and all set in a world where you could tell a character's intentions by their clothes.

Leo had rolled his eyes at first, berating the film because it was never like that in the real world. If you could just tell the villains from the heroes by the way they appeared, then everything would be far easier.

Yet, then again, maybe there was some truth in that. Leo hadn't liked Andy from the first time they'd met. Leo never thought the man was dangerous. He was just patronizing, arrogant, a bully, and generally not a nice person to spend time with.

The fact Leo's sister had chosen to have a relationship with the guy had confused Leo. When she said they were getting married, Leo really was baffled.

A car flipped over on the screen, and a group of people ran for cover. Leo wondered what happened to the evil characters after the heroes won.

Although Leo was confident that they could find a man like Andy, he was less optimistic that Andy would ever be the man that his sister and nephew deserved.

Ninety minutes later, the plane having landed, and laborious immigration checks done, Leo and Allissa climbed out of the taxi and gazed across the Hudson River. The iconic towers of Manhattan soared into the cerulean afternoon sky.

"This is it?" Leo asked the taxi driver as they stopped outside a large and modern apartment building on Wellington Avenue.

"That's the one." The driver pointed at the building's grand entrance.

Leo paid the taxi with his credit card, wincing at the price. They wouldn't usually take a taxi that distance, but today time was short.

Allissa thanked the driver, got out, and stared up at the building. "Cool place," she said.

Andy's brother, Michael, was waiting for them as the elevator doors opened.

"We came back as soon as we heard," Michael said. "Left the kids at the parents' in Orlando. We just want to be here for Em."

Leo had only met Michael once, at Emma and Andy's wedding.

Michael was clearly Andy's brother. They looked alike, except Michael kept his sandy hair in a messy style and wore thick-framed glasses.

"Good to see you again," Michael said, shaking Leo's hand. "Shame it's in these circumstances."

Leo introduced Allissa, then Michael led them into the apartment.

"Thank you for coming so quickly," Michael said. "The police are looking too, but I know you guys are experts at this. I've been following your cases. Impressive stuff."

Leo and Allissa followed Michael through a brightly lit hallway and into the apartment's open-plan living space.

"Great place," Allissa said, spinning around. She gazed out the windows at the city skyline. "And check out that view."

Michael smiled weakly.

Emma stood from the sofa where she had been sitting with Michael's wife, Nadia. All exchanged hugs and greetings.

"We came as quickly as we could," Leo said, taking his sister in his arms.

"Thank you, thank you." Emma pushed her face into Leo's shoulder.

Holding Emma, Leo realized how frail and vulnerable she had become. Anger at the man who'd caused this pain welled up inside him.

Emma took a deep breath and pulled away. "I'm sorry for calling you. I just didn't know what else to do."

"Don't be sorry," Allissa said. "This is what we do. We want to help you."

Emma nodded and retook her seat on the sofa. When the introductions and niceties were complete, Leo sunk into the sofa beside his sister. Allissa took a seat in one of the armchairs and consulted the notes on her phone.

"Is there anything we can do to help you?" Michael asked, his gaze moving between Leo and Allissa.

"We just need to know as much as possible," Allissa told him. "That'll give us the best chance of finding Andy."

Emma stared morosely down at her fingers.

Getting down to business, Allissa went through what they knew already.

"That's it exactly," Emma said. "The police woke me up, and he wasn't here. I'd taken a pill to help me sleep after the jet lag and didn't hear anything."

"What did he take with him?" Allissa asked.

Nadia straightened up uncomfortably.

"Nothing, really. His suitcase is here. He took some of Michael's clothes, that's it."

"Is his passport here?" Leo asked.

Emma nodded.

Nadia squirmed.

"Wallet? Credit cards? Money?" Allissa said.

"Nope, all here."

"He can't have gone that far then," Leo said. "He wouldn't be able to afford—"

"You've got to tell them," Nadia declared, staring at Michael.

Michael glanced at her. If the interjection annoyed him, he didn't show it.

"Tell us what?" Allissa asked.

"Okay," Michael said, putting a hand on his wife's forearm. "We didn't tell the police because I didn't want Andy to be in any more trouble. Honestly, it doesn't matter. Andy took the cash we keep in the apartment for emergencies."

"How much?"

"Two thousand dollars," Nadia cut in.

"It's not a problem at all," Michael said. "Of course, we'd have given it to him if he'd asked. Wouldn't we Nadia?"

Leo glanced from husband to wife. It didn't look as though Nadia seemed so sure.

"Okay, thanks for telling us that," Allissa said. "That changes the sort of places we'll look."

"He took your car as well?" Leo asked.

"Yes. We assume so, at least. Police found the car around two in the morning in the Lincoln Tunnel. Totally smashed up. Unrecognizable. Much to their surprise, it was empty. How anyone could've walked away from a wreck like that, they didn't know."

Emma sobbed and dabbed at her face with a tissue.

Allissa made a note of the time and location.

"We're not worried about the car, or the money," Michael confirmed. "We just want to know where Andy is."

Nadia crossed her arms and turned away from her husband. A few frosty seconds of silence passed.

"I think we have everything we need," Allissa said, standing from the chair. "We will get out of your way and make a start."

"Are you sure?" Michael said. "Stay for dinner, we will get something..."

"Honestly, it's fine," Allissa said. "You've got enough going on here. You guys look after Emma, and we will get down to this."

Leo climbed to his feet, gave Emma another hug and stepped toward the door. Leo looked at Emma. He wanted to stay with her, but Andy wouldn't get found that way.

"We'll look after her, don't worry," Nadia said, clearly aware of Leo's turmoil. "You go find Andy as we all want a word with him."

"Is there anything we can do to help?" Michael said, showing Leo and Allissa to the door. "Do you need somewhere to stay?"

"We booked a place yesterday, but thanks," Leo said.

"We've got everything we need to get started," Allissa confirmed, pulling open the door.

"Okay," Michael said. He looked away, and then suddenly a thought occurred to him. "If you need a bit of local help, a friend of ours recommended a private investigator a while ago." Michael glanced at Nadia. "What was that detective called?"

"Niki Zadid," Nadia said.

"Yes, that was it. I can look up the contact details for you now if you..."

"Got it," Allissa said, running a quick internet search. "That's a useful recommendation, thank you. Having a person who knows the area is always helpful."

"I can imagine. And I'm paying the bill. No arguments about that."

"Sure." Leo hugged Nadia and shook Michael's hand. "We'll be in touch soon. If you think of anything else that might be useful, let us know."

11

———

LOCAL KNOWLEDGE COUNTED for everything when trying to track someone down. Cases were lost or won on what you knew about the location and its people.

"I'm not saying we shouldn't get help," Leo said as the metro rumbled beneath Manhattan. "I just think we should think about what we can do on our own first."

"No," Allissa said. "We can't afford to waste time. We need to get this detective on the case as soon as possible. He'll know where to look. He'll have all the contacts. Remember when you were looking for me in Kathmandu? What was the first thing you did?"

"Okay," Leo conceded. Allissa was right. The first thing he'd done on arriving in Kathmandu was contact someone who knew the city, the local customs, and could speak the language. Tau had been invaluable. Leo likely wouldn't have found Allissa or survived the ordeal without him.

"What do we know about this detective, then?" Leo asked as Allissa thumbed the bell of Niki Zadid's office in Greenwich Village. The office was on the third floor of a townhouse in a wide, quiet, and tree-lined street. The area felt a long way from the famous spires of the Empire State and Chrysler buildings, which pierced the skyline to the north, and the World Trade Center, which cast its long shadow from the south.

"Not a lot, really. But Michael recommended him. His website lists all sorts of things, marital stuff, missing people, research for legal cases, that sort of thing."

A taxi hissed beneath the skeletal trees behind them. Allissa stepped back and stared up at the four-story building. To their left, people sat at the outside tables of a café, despite the cold.

"Maybe he's not in," Leo said. "He might be out on a case or something. You know, chasing down criminals. We should have got an appointment."

"Yeah, that's probably true. We were passing anyway, though. Let's try again."

Leo jabbed at the buzzer once more. He leaned in and pressed his ear against the door, straining to catch the sound of the bell. Music boomed from somewhere inside. A pulsating beat throbbed through walls and windows.

Leo shifted his weight further forward still, his ear tight against the glass. Deep inside, one song ended, and another began with renewed vigor.

Without warning, the door clicked and swung open. Leo's body tipped forward, and he stumbled inside.

His arms flailed, trying to grab something to arrest his fall. His fingers swept through the air, clawing at nothing. Off balance, he fell through the open door and crashed into a woman coming the other way.

"Watch where you're going, will ya!" the woman said, clearly not expecting to get an arm full of an unkempt and confused English detective.

"Sorry, sorry!" Leo said. He pulled himself upright and immediately blushed.

Allissa tried and failed to stifle a laugh.

The woman took a step back and scrutinized Leo for a long second, as though trying to decide what to do with him. Eventually, she scowled, brushed herself down, pushed between Leo and Allissa and stomped away.

"I said that we should get on with the locals, not throw ourselves at them," Allissa quipped.

Leo barked out a dry laugh as the blood finally drained from his face.

"Quick, grab that," Allissa said, pointing at the door, which was swinging closed.

Leo slid his foot between the door and the jamb just in time to stop the lock engaging.

"I know you'll say that we haven't got an appointment, but let's just check that Niki Zadid isn't in the office." Allissa swung the door open again and strode inside.

"I suppose." Leo shrugged and followed Allissa into a grand hallway. "A locked door has never stopped us before."

A brass sign on the wall advised that N. Zadid's office was on the third floor. Following Allissa up the stairs, Leo thought of their flat's stuffy entrance hall. At home, piles of junk mail and rusting bikes welcomed Leo and Allissa's prospective clients. In stark contrast Niki Zadid's building was furnished with ornate mirrors and a sleek tiled floor.

"Maybe we should get a place like this," Allissa said, turning and catching Leo's eye.

Leo nodded in agreement.

As Leo and Allissa climbed the stairs, the music became louder still. The deep thud of a kick drum and a bouncing bassline reminded Leo of the club they'd visited a few weeks ago in Berlin. On the third floor, the walls shook from thumping bass. A black and white framed photograph of a group of men unloading a train bounced against its fixings.

Allissa paused and turned to face Leo. Another brass sign beside the door indicated that they had found the office of *N. Zadid P.I.*

The music was coming from inside.

Leo pointed at the sign. "I'm sort of disappointed the writing isn't on a glass door like in all the famous detective novels."

Allissa rolled her eyes. "You think Niki will be in there with his feet on the desk, smoking a cigar and drinking whiskey?"

"If he's not, I'm going to be both surprised and disappointed," Leo said.

Allissa knocked on the door, but the grunting bass masked the sound. Unsurprisingly, there was no response. Allissa tried again, this time rapping on the door as hard as she could. Nothing happened for a moment, and then the music stopped.

Leo and Allissa glanced at each other. The door didn't move. Allissa knocked again.

"Come in!" boomed a voice from inside.

Allissa pushed open the door and stepped into the room. Prints of modern art covered the pastel blue walls. A crystal chandelier glittered on the ceiling. Bookshelves covered the wall at one end of the room, and windows overlooked the street at the other. Sumptuous sofas gathered around a glass table. On the table, a map and a few documents were the only indication Leo had of the occupant's profession.

"Can I help you?" came a female voice in a bold New York accent.

Leo and Allissa spun around to see a woman slide an

enormous book from one of the shelves. She casually flicked the book open and leafed through without even looking up at her intruders. She paused on a page and then tapped the book thoughtfully.

The woman was slight, short, moved with bird-like efficiency and wore a bright blue hijab which covered her hair and flowed down her back. Her clothes, although modest, had a fashionable cut. She gave the impression that nothing about her appearance was an accident.

"Yes, I hope so," Leo said. "We're looking for Niki Zadid."

"Why?" the woman snapped in reply. Still not looking directly at Leo or Allissa, the woman crossed the room and laid the book on the table.

"We're missing people investigators," Allissa told her. "We're looking for someone here in New York and could do with a bit of help."

The woman flicked forward two pages, then finally glanced at Leo and Allissa.

"Sorry to be pushy," Leo said. "We'd rather just talk to Niki about this, if possible. Time really is…"

"Is this guy having a joke?" the woman said, locking eyes with Allissa but throwing a nod toward Leo. "You wanna talk to Niki, huh?" She stood upright and placed her hands on her hips. "Who do you think you're looking at?"

Allissa laughed out loud, and Niki's expression broke into a lopsided grin. Leo blushed.

Leo mumbled a few words, blushing profusely. "I'm so sorry," he said, finally, managing to get over this embarrassment.

"Leave it, Sherlock," Niki cut in. "A lesson for the future, though, you go into an office with a name on the door, and the person you're most likely to find there is…" Niki pointed at Leo. "It's not a trick question," she continued before Leo had the chance to reply.

Leo tried to apologize again, but Niki stopped him with a raised hand.

"Now stop apologizing. I know I don't look the part. Let me guess, you were expecting a middle-aged, cigar smoking man, probably also halfway through a bottle of whiskey."

"Of course not," Leo said, throwing Allissa a look which gave no doubt that any comments from her were not at all welcome. "I just wasn't…"

"You know, it's probably what makes me good at my job. No one expects this." Niki tugged on her hijab. "Now, I don't know about you, but my detective work involves too many late nights and not enough sleep."

"Tell me about that. We only flew in a few hours ago and were up late last night," Allissa said.

"The way I see it, there are two things you can do about that." Niki nodded knowingly. "Take a week off to sit on the beach, or drink strong coffee by the bucket load." Niki pointed a finger at Leo. "Which one of those do you think I'm going to offer you now, detective?"

"I don't think I'm ready for another beach," Allissa added, almost silently.

"Coffee, definitely," Leo said.

Niki clapped her hands and strode toward the sort of coffee machine, which would fit right in on the counter of a specialist café.

"I would ask you how you take your coffee, but I only make it one way." Niki jabbed a few buttons, and the machine hissed and spat. The rich scent of fresh coffee drifted through the room. Niki filled three cups and carried them to the table.

"You have a beautiful office," Allissa said, accepting the cup and sinking into one of the luxurious sofas.

"Thanks. Yeah, I do alright. There are a lot of rich people in this city, and rich people don't trust each other. It seems they spend half their time trying to make money and the other half worrying about losing it. So, they hire me."

"That sounds good to me," Leo said. He took a sip of the bitter but beautifully rich coffee.

"It's not bad. I can't complain. I've been doing this for ten years now. I tell you this, it's not all it's cracked up to be. I thought I'd be tracking down murderers, or reuniting missing people, but most of the work I tend to get is from suspicious husbands or wives."

"I can understand that," Allissa said. "We tend to specialize in people who go missing, but of course things end up being more complicated and dangerous than you'd expect."

"A suspicious husband or wife doesn't sound bad at all," Leo said. "Less than twenty-four hours ago we had to flee a group of mercenaries. I'm pretty sure they would have buried our bodies in the forest if we hadn't got away."

Niki's eyes widened, and she looked from one detective to the other.

"It's not exactly like that," Allissa said. "Leo has a very dramatic way of phrasing things."

"Only speaking the truth." Leo shrugged.

"That sounds exciting to me. It sounds much more fun than following Mrs. Fitzwater's husband for the fifth time this year, even though she pays very well."

"That's clearly true," Allissa said, looking around at the office.

"How can I help you, then?" Niki said, finishing the coffee and leaning back into the sofa. Looking at the woman, Leo thought it seemed as though her personality occupied more space than she did physically.

Allissa carefully explained the situation.

"You got a name?" Niki said.

"Yeah, Andy Harris," Allissa said. "Here are a few recent pictures."

Niki dug a wafer-thin laptop from beneath a map on the table and opened it. The laptop was about a third the size of Allissa's. "Send me that picture," Niki said, her fingers flashing over the keys.

While the women got to work, Leo glanced at the map on the table, which displayed a section of Manhattan. Niki had marked the map with two crosses and a pile of books about famous serial killers lay open to one side. Although the display piqued Leo's curiosity, he resisted the urge to ask.

"Describe this Andy character to me," Niki said, tapping on the keys.

Leo gave Niki all the background information he thought was relevant.

Niki's phone beeped, and she grabbed it from the tabletop.

"Sorry," Niki said, "I've just gotta check this." She tapped a few keys, and a large screen on the wall blazed to life. Footage of a young man with a wave of brown hair and intense gray eyes materialized on the screen. A television news reporter asked the man a series of questions.

"How does he know so much?" Niki muttered.

"What's that?" Allissa asked.

"Two girls were murdered last night, and it looks like the work of a serial killer. They've already named him the Downtown Ripper." Niki pointed at the screen. "This guy writes a true crime blog. The fact that the press is all over him means the police haven't released any information…"

"Which probably means the police don't know anything," Leo said.

Niki's grin lit her face again, and she pointed at Leo. "My thoughts exactly," she said. "We will have to wait and see what happens."

"Wait a second." Leo broke Niki's gaze and glanced again at the books and map on the table. "You're looking into this, aren't you?"

"Too right I am," Niki said, jabbing at the map. "If I can break this before the NYPD, then I won't have to do the bidding of suspicious housewives ever again."

The man on the screen spoke for a couple more minutes, and then the news anchorman reappeared.

"Alright," Niki said, turning off the television and flashing Leo and Allissa a grin. "Let's go find this brother of yours." She placed her hands on her knees.

"He's my brother in law," Leo muttered. "And we're going now? Don't you…"

"Of course we're going now!" Niki said. "I've no idea how you do things across the pond, but here in NYC things move quick. If we want to find this guy. We need to move now."

12

———

"Axel!" Niki shouted, banging on a door between a second-hand clothes shop and a launderette. The only customer in either was a young Chinese man staring morosely at his spinning clothes.

They'd left Niki's office nearly an hour ago, walked across Greenwich Village, and rode the subway over to Queens. Leo found the bubbling noise of the city disconcerting as he followed Niki through the subway station's crowds and back out into the sunlight.

"Axel!" Niki pounded the door again. The door shook against its fixings. Leo was surprised by Niki's strength and aggression.

"Who's Axel?" Leo asked, looking around the dingy street to which Niki had led them.

"Let me explain." Niki turned and eyed Leo and then Allissa. "New York's had a big homeless community since the great depression. To this day, more and more people arrive thinking the city holds the answers they need. There are around sixty-thousand homeless people in this city alone."

"But how does that help…"

"If there's one way to stay out of sight in New York, it's within the homeless community. The police will have already checked hotel records and that sort of thing. The only way Andy could remain un-detected in New York is to go underground, as it were."

"Good point," Leo said. "And Axel?"

"Axel understands this world better than anyone I know. If Andy's in that world, Axel will know about it. If he doesn't know himself, he will know who to ask."

"He sounds like a good person to know," Allissa added.

"He is," Niki said. "But he don't just talk to anyone. With Axel you gotta treat him in a certain way to get answers." Niki stopped talking to hammer on the door again. The door rattled against the jamb, giving Leo the illusion that at any point it was in danger of bursting inwards.

"I suppose that's why we couldn't just call him on the phone?" Leo murmured.

"Exactly that," Niki replied. "You wanna know what's going on in this city, Axel's your guy. Axel!" Niki shouted yet again, followed by another staccato against the wood.

Niki was about to hammer again when the door swung open. A three-inch gap which showed only gloom appeared between the door and the jamb.

"What you want?" A young woman with bleary eyes appeared. She elongated the word *waaaaant*, lending the question the tone of a stubborn teenager.

"Axel in?" Niki said, her tone cutting through the stale air of the dimly lit hallway.

"Who you?" The voice lacked any real challenge. The woman slouched against the peeling frame, her clothes baggy and stained.

"We're friends of Axel." Niki gestured casually toward Leo and Allissa, who stood a step behind.

"I didn't know Axel had any friends," the self-appointed, although lackluster gatekeeper said. Her gaze shifted lazily from Leo to Allissa and then back to Niki. Her gaze betrayed neither interest nor concern.

"There's an ocean of things you don't know," Niki hissed, her words steely. "Are you going to open the door, or do we have to discuss this further?"

Clearly sensing the insistence in Niki's tone and the set of her jaw, the reluctant gatekeeper moved aside and released the door.

Niki stepped into the shadowy interior, her boots thudding on the bare, worn floorboards. Leo and Allissa followed her into a foyer where the wallpaper hung in defeated strips.

The air inside was thick with the musty scent of damp and decay. They passed under an archway, the plaster crumbled at the edges. Sparse, flickering lightbulbs cast more shadow than illumination, creating a dance of gloom and light throughout the hallway.

Niki strode toward the staircase with Leo and Allissa two steps behind. As they ascended, the stairs creaked under their weight. Halfway up, the landing above came into view. The wallpaper here was not just peeling but hanging in long tongue-like strips. A bare bulb flickered above them, its feeble light struggling to penetrate the gloom.

As they reached the top of the stairs, a door swung open, and a tiny man bounded out.

"Niki!" he shouted, his arms raised as though in praise. "It's good to see ya!"

Niki grinned and strode toward the small man. The pair

merged into a hug, whispering some words that Leo couldn't make out. Niki introduced Leo and Allissa with a formality that would have been more suitable to an executive office.

"Step inside, don't just stand there." Axel beckoned with a casual wave. Niki entered with a nod, her silhouette framed briefly in the doorway before stepping into the dimly lit room. Leo and Allissa followed.

Out on the landing, the thought hadn't occurred to Leo that they were stepping into Axel's bedroom. Once inside, Leo felt as though he was intruding. He looked around at the narrow bed, covered by crumpled, greying sheets, the simple desk in the corner, cluttered with papers and various aged electronics. The main feature of the room, however, were the well-packed shelves which lined almost all available wall space.

"How have ya been?" Niki asked, sitting on a box by the door.

"Oh, you know." Axel flicked his wrist. "I'm getting by. Taking each day as it comes sorta thing."

Niki nodded.

"Sit down, sit down," Axel said, pointing Leo and Allissa toward the bed. They sat down, eliciting a creak from the lumpy bed.

Axel leapt onto a small and threadbare office chair.

"Niki got this place for me," Axel said with evident pride. "If it wasn't for her, I'd be out there somewhere. God knows where." His legs wiggled as he spoke. Even on the little chair, they hung without touching the floor. "We'd built it up all nice. It was a place just for us. Our own. Then the city wanted to take it back and turn it back into some kind of hotel. No one would help me, other than her." He pointed at Niki with both hands. "My angel."

"It wasn't really like that," Niki said. "I just pointed you in the right direction. You did most of the hard work yourselves."

"Nonsense, if we hadn't had your firm's backing..."

"I was a property lawyer at the time," Niki explained. "That was over fifteen years ago now."

"That it was." Axel nodded, his expression grave. "And not a day goes by that I'm not thankful for it." The small man looked at Leo and Allissa. "I just didn't know what to do. Then Niki just came out of the darkness."

"Now you're being dramatic," Niki said, taking over the story. "Axel contacted me because they couldn't pay the legal fees, so the city was just going to take ownership."

"We ended up buying it for one dollar, and now it's ours." Axel waved his short arms to demonstrate the breadth of his kingdom.

"What're you doing here?" Niki pointed to the boxes strewn across the floor.

Axel straightened his bright yellow necktie.

"In these boxes," Axel said with grandeur, "are photos from thirty years of living in this and other squats around the city. From us first breaking in." He pulled a picture from a pile and showed it to his audience. It was a gritty black and white print of an empty derelict room. "Renovating it." He produced another picture in which two men grinned toward the camera from a scaffold tower. "Oh, and this is my favorite." He reached for a photograph propped against a tin. "Before we went legal, we used to have gigs down where the shop now is. Bands would play just for their board. This is *The Pistons*. It was before they got big, obviously." In the picture, dark shapes swayed amongst the grains of black and white. "There are some from the day we officially became legal too," Axel continued, his legs wiggling constantly with excitement. "There might even be one with you in it." He pointed at Niki.

"What're you doing with them?" Allissa asked.

Axel turned to her with a look of pantomime surprise.

"Why, cataloging and digitizing them, of course!" He gestured toward the dirty gray computer and scanner on the table beside him. A piece of masking tape covered the computer's built-in webcam.

"This is an important record of social history," Axel said. "This is our history. Galleries across the world would be interested in this."

"These photos are great," Niki said, flicking through a pile.

"I know," Axel said. "This is my life's work, and now this place is secure, I can concentrate on telling my story. But you didn't come here to talk about that!" Axel said abruptly. He turned to face Leo and Allissa.

"We're looking for his brother," Niki said, nodding at Leo.

"Brother-in-law," Leo interjected.

"I see. Tell me all."

Allissa explained the situation and Axel listened quietly.

"And you want to know where he might be hiding beneath the radar, so to speak," Axel said, proudly slipping his thumbs into his belt.

"If that's possible," Leo replied.

"There's no knowing of course," Axel said. "But I'll see what I can do. Where was he last seen?"

"The car crash happened in the Lincoln Tunnel, just fifty feet from the Manhattan end. Our guess is he was able to climb out and disappear into the city before the emergency crews arrived," Allissa said.

"Let me see what I can do," Axel muttered, the muscles

in his face tensing with thought. "It really is very interesting," Axel continued, tapping his chin. "If memory serves, there are several places in stumbling distance of there. Niki honey, pass me that map there." He pointed to a shelf above Niki's head.

Niki passed Axel the rolled-up map. Axel hopped down from his seat and spread it across the floor. Niki shuffled her box backward to make space, but even then, the room was too small to show the entire thing.

Leo recognized it as a map of Manhattan, covered in various markings made in felt tip pens in a range of colors.

"Look, here we are. Here's the entrance to the Lincoln tunnel." Axel stabbed at the map with a small finger. "So your brother was there at some point yesterday morning."

"Brother-in-law," Leo groaned.

"Yes, that's what I said," Axel continued. "Now, there are a few places around there, in stumbling distance at least. But I would say, with a good deal of certainty, that he ended up here." Axel poked at the map again.

Leo leaned forward and noticed that the place Axel indicated had been marked with a blue cross.

"What is that place?" Allissa said, beating Leo to the question.

"That is a disused underground parking lot. A lot of my contacts use it to get out of the bad weather. Of course, they would prefer it on the street, out in the open air. Sometimes, however, even free spirits have to shelter from the rain.

Leo studied the map in reserved disbelief. Although it would be incredible if this man knew where Andy had gone just from looking at a dusty map, Leo wasn't hopeful. He glanced up at Niki, who sat with her legs crossed and her back straight. So far, she seemed like a skillful detective. If she believed Axel, then maybe there was some truth in it.

"That's where your brother stayed last night, I'm telling you," Axel said.

"Brother-in..." Leo moaned.

"If I was a betting man, I'd put money on it. Or if I had any money to begin with," Axel added.

"Then that's where we'll start looking," Allissa said, climbing to her feet.

13

____

"This is it," Niki said an hour later as they paced down a narrow ramp and into an underground parking lot. The third floor was beneath street level and beneath a bus station. The place wasn't exactly easy to find.

"I'm not confident," Leo said, glancing around at the bare concrete walls. "I can't understand how Andy will have found this place."

"If you're looking for a place to stay for the night, then you become pretty resourceful," Niki replied, her voice carrying a hard edge.

"True, I suppose, but Andy was blind drunk, remember? He drove the car into the wall of the tunnel," Leo countered.

"Even more so then," Niki said. "He will have been running on instinct." Niki stopped and turned to face Leo. "If you wanna do this on your own, then go ahead. I know this city, and I know how to find people here."

"No, we appreciate your help," Allissa said to Niki. She turned and burned a hole in the side of Leo's face with a _shut up and let me handle this_ glare.

"Fine, then follow me," Niki commanded, her voice echoing in the cavernous space as she retrieved a small flashlight from her bag and clicked it on. The beam cut through the dimness as they descended further along the curving ramp. Their footsteps echoed, a staccato rhythm bouncing off the concrete walls, while in the distance, the steady plunk of water droplets striking stone punctuated the silence, like the methodical ticking of a clock.

Arriving at the lowest level of the underground car park, they moved beneath a flickering fluorescent light that cast an erratic, otherworldly glow. Shadows jumped and retreated with each pulse of the faulty bulb, creating a disorienting dance of light and darkness.

Niki swept her flashlight around the space, although Leo couldn't see anything but an abandoned expanse. It was strange to think about the city thriving above this forgotten space.

Niki led them deeper into the vast expanse of the car park. The further they walked, the darker the space seemed to become, swallowing the weak beam of Niki's flashlight like a supernova.

To Leo, the vast open space felt unsettling and desolate. It wasn't dissimilar, he remembered, to the abandoned Berlin Spy station in which they'd almost lost their lives just weeks ago.

As they walked, the silence was a tangible presence, only broken by the distant drip of water and their own footsteps.

"Look, there," Niki hissed, focusing her light on something against a wall twenty feet away. They paced closer and saw the telltale signs of human habitation. Several sleeping bags were strewn haphazardly across the cold floor, empty bottles that once held booze lay in a pile alongside the remnants of food packets.

"Hey, what you doin' down here?" came a baritone voice, echoing through the space.

Niki spun on her heel, the flashlight's beam cutting through the gloom, and caught sight of a slender figure unsteadily approaching them through the shadows.

"You guys got no business down here. This place ain't for the likes of you."

"We're looking for someone," Leo said. "I wonder if..."

"There ain't no one to be found down here," the guy said, taking another step forward. The man was tall, two or three inches over six feet. His eyes whipped from side to side, assessing the intruders.

"I think you can help us," Niki said, taking charge. "And there'll be some money in it for you, if you can."

The guy stopped, and his brow furrowed. "How much?" He said, his gaze hardening.

"Ten dollars?" Leo replied, earning himself a subtle dig in the ribs from Allissa.

"Ten dollars!" The man bellowed. "What am I supposed to do with ten dollars? You wanna buy me a lollipop?"

"I'll give fifty for anything you can tell us that's worth knowing," Niki offered, deftly manifesting the banknote with a flourish that bordered on the magical.

The man took a few plodding steps forward, his hand outstretched.

"No, you don't," Niki said, withdrawing the note. "You talk to us first, then you'll get this."

The man grumbled for a few seconds and then conceded. "What you need to know?"

"We're looking for his brother," Niki said, nodding toward Leo.

Leo was about to correct the statement but got an icy

glare from Allissa telling him that now certainly wasn't the time to be pedantic.

"He was in an accident the night before last near here. No one's seen him. We figure he may have found his way down here, or one of you guys might have brought him down here. Being the good Samaritans, you are and all that."

The man puffed out his cheeks and his eye balls did another circuit of the parking lot.

"Here's a picture of him," Allissa said, passing her phone across.

The man peered at the photograph with a casual interest that soon gave way to intense scrutiny. His pupils dilating with the shock of familiarity. A jolt of surprise sent him reeling back slightly, the soles of his shoes scraping against the floor as he steadied himself.

"You recognize him, don't you?" Niki said, watching him closely.

"Maybe I do," the guy said, his eyes moving even more frantically than before. "Money now and I'll tell ya."

Niki stared at the man for three whole seconds. She raised a hand with the note pinned between her outstretched fingers and pointed at the man. "Fine, but you mess with me, and it'll be the last thing you do."

The man swiped at the note, but Niki drew it out of the way with the speed of a viper.

"You hear me?" she said. "You mess with me, and I'll come for you."

"Sure thing," the man said, swiping at the note again. This time, Niki let him take it.

"Start talking," she said, folding her arms.

"That guy was here. I remember him. Eddie, one of the

guys who lives here, saw him out on the street. Your man, what's his name?"

"Andy," Allissa offered.

"Andy looked like the sort of guy with nowhere to go. People like us recognize things like that. Anyway, Eddie gets talking to him, and Andy says he's got a bit of cash but doesn't want to go to a hotel on his own. Eddie says that if he buys a few bottles, Andy can come down here and spend a few hours."

"You're sure it was him?" Niki said.

"Yes, absolutely. He stayed a few hours, we all have a drink, then he finally passes out. But the problem is, he doesn't sleep. He's there shouting all night long. He's shoutin' for someone called Emma."

Leo and Allissa exchanged a glance at the mention of Emma's name. Leo was thankful that the gloom hid his surprise that Axel's lead had paid off.

"Is he still there?" Niki said.

"No, thankfully," the man said, gurgling out a laugh. "After a few hours, we're all so sick of him we tell Eddie he gotta wake the guy up and chuck him out. Eddie says it's not his fault the guy ended up being crazy. We say that Eddie bought him here..."

"What happened then?" Niki said, trying to get the information back on to the topic.

"Eddie wakes him up and walks him back up to the street and sends him on his way," the man said, finally.

"Do you know where he went from here?" Allissa said.

The man spun around and looked at Allissa as though noticing her for the first time.

"Yeah, Andy wanted to do some more boozing. Said he didn't ever want to stop."

"That sounds like him," Leo muttered.

"We told him about a bar not far from here that's open 24 hours a day. He said he was gonna go there and stormed off. No thanks to any of us for accommodating him."

"That sounds like him, too," Leo added.

"What bar is that?" Niki asked.

"Maddison's," the man said. "We told him to go to Maddison's Corner Café."

TONIGHT, things were going to go down a little differently. He was going to enjoy tonight even more. He looked at himself in the mirror and smiled. He knew he had a certain look about him. A look that got him a lot of attention. The right kind of attention. And tonight, he was going to use that to his advantage.

Although the plan last night had worked — he had, after all, found two women and done what he'd wanted — he hadn't been able to *choose* them. He'd got lucky with the first one. She had been beautiful.

He closed his eyes and pictured her naked porcelain figure. The image hadn't left his mind all day. He ran his fingers across the bracelet on his left wrist and bit his lower lip. He wanted them all to look like that. He *needed* them to look like that.

The problem was, if he simply lay in wait for someone to pass, then he just had to take whoever turned up. There was too much luck involved. He didn't know who was going to pass, nor whether they would be to his specific tastes.

This way, he thought, pulling on his blazer, he got to choose exactly who he wanted.

It was unusual for a serial killer to change their M.O. like this. But, that was the beauty of it. He could slip through the doors of the city's bars and clubs, and no one would think twice. That was better than hiding in an alleyway and waiting for a victim. This way, he could choose carefully. He could select someone he wanted to spend time with.

He brought the gold bracelet to his mouth and kissed it.

"I'll make you proud," he whispered.

14

———

LEO AND ALISSA followed Niki along New York's jam-packed sidewalks. Walking a few steps ahead, Niki swerved through the crowds as though she knew instinctively how people would move in advance. Leo and Allissa, on the other hand, continually found themselves stopping behind people who wanted to gaze in shop windows or darting around those coming the other way.

Five minutes later, Niki dropped her pace, allowing the non-New Yorkers to catch up. Matching pace with Niki, Leo noticed she was on the phone. Niki spoke for half a block and then ended the call.

"A client, I'm afraid." She threw Leo and Allissa a glance. "You guys will be alright for a few hours, right? You know what you're doing?"

"Of course," Allissa said, thanking Niki for her help so far.

"You can't miss it," Niki said, pointing them in the direction of Maddison's Corner Café. "Just up there and you'll see it." Niki swerved seamlessly down the steps and into a metro station.

Leo glanced up at the darkening sky as they settled into a slightly less frantic pace toward the place where Andy had last been seen. Or at least, he reminded himself, the place someone had told him to go.

"I have to confess, I thought Axel's lead would get us nowhere," Leo said.

"You think he just made it up?" Allissa said, smirking.

"I wouldn't go so far as to say he made it up," Leo said, backtracking slightly. "He didn't seem like a deceitful guy…"

"But?" Allissa interrupted.

"This city has millions of people in it." Leo swept his arm around, indicating the packed sidewalk. "Sorry if I didn't believe it was possible for him to know the exact place Andy staggered into."

"It did seem unlikely," Allissa admitted. "But Niki knows what she's doing. She wouldn't have wasted time going all the way to visit Axel if he spoke nonsense."

"That is true," Leo said.

"But you were right." Allissa held out her hands, as though surrendering to Leo's logic. "This could all be a wild goose chase."

"We're quickly becoming experts at chasing wild geese," Leo muttered.

"There it is!" Allissa said, pointing across an intersection. Madison's Corner Café occupied the corner of the opposite block. Adverts above the door promised sports, beer, live music, food, twenty-four-hours a day.

"Just looking at that place is giving me a headache," Leo moaned. Darkened windows hinted at activity inside, without displaying what such activity might involve. Leo knew, before they were even close to the place, that it would be loud.

The lights changed and Leo and Allissa crossed the

street with at least a hundred other people. They pushed their way through the crowd coming the other way and finally reached the door to the café. Leo held the door open for Allissa, and the pair stepped into the bar's cavernous interior.

Leo winced at the thumping music, then did a three-sixty of the venue. Sport and news played on half a dozen giant screens, countless beer taps sparkled on the bar, and a spectrum of bottles gleamed from the back bar. The air conditioner kicked out hot air and rock-pop hits of the nineties bellowed from the speakers.

Allissa weaved her way through the crowd and slipped on to one of the stools at the bar. Leo followed.

"This is exactly the place I can see Andy coming," Leo said, bright lights and noise already making him uncomfortable.

"If it involves booze, I think he'd go anywhere," Allissa replied.

Leo peered up at the screen directly above them, which was tuned to a news channel. Viewed as a whole, the array of screens blurred into a single, overwhelming tapestry of global life — ball games, statistics, crises, and politics, all jumbled together into an indistinguishable mess.

He focused on a news channel's icon spinning on the screen just above him. The graphics faded, and a broad-shouldered anchor-man appeared.

As the anchorman narrated the story, the caption *Downtown Ripper Takes Third Victim* scrolled across the bottom of the screen. The news report transitioned abruptly, the screen filling with the grim tableau of an active crime scene. The familiar, jarring sight of yellow tape billowed in the breeze, cordoning off a narrow alleyway.

"Leo, hello?" Allissa said, drawing Leo's attention away from the unfolding story.

"Sorry, was just watching that." He pointed at the screen. "It's the Downtown Ripper story that Niki was talking about. It looks bad. That's three people this guy has killed now."

The camera zoomed out to reveal the diner beside which the body had been found. The news report rolled onto the next story. A man wearing white gloves held a gun, and a flag flew at half-staff.

"Get you a drink?" hollered the bartender, stretching over the counter to speak over the booming music.

"I wonder if you can help me with something," Allissa said. "We're looking for a friend of ours. We think he was in here last night. Were you working last night?"

"I was working last night, yes," the barman confirmed. "Haven't had a night off in... I can't even remember." He leaned further across the bar, his face just inches from Allissa's cheek.

"Great, you might be able to help us then." Allissa's fingers swiped across her phone, bringing up a photo of Andy. She held the device out toward the barman. "We're looking for this guy and think he might have been here last night. It's a real long shot."

The barman took the phone, his eyes narrowing as he studied the photograph.

Leo and Allissa watched the man like a hawk, unable to read his gestures. For several seconds the barman gazed hard at the photograph.

"You know what? I do recognize him," the barman said, pointing at the picture.

"Wait, what?" Allissa said, unsure whether she'd heard him correctly above the din.

"I said, I do recognize him." The barman leaned over

again. "I'm almost certain of it. He came in on his own and sat at the bar for a while. Then he ended up drinking with Otto, one of our regulars. I finished at four am, and he was still here."

Allissa examined the man in disbelief.

"Okay," Allissa said, concentrating. "Did you notice anything strange about him?"

"No, not really. Just a normal guy." The barman handed Allissa's phone back and folded his arms.

"Do you remember what he was wearing?" Leo said, his voice cracking as he tried to talk over the noise.

"Nah, not really. Shirt and jeans maybe."

"How do we find this guy he was chatting to? The regular."

The door clattered open, and a blast of cold air streamed in from the street. Allissa glanced across. A large man wearing jeans, a red shirt, and a wide-brimmed Stetson lumbered into the bar. The steel heels of his boots clacked across the wooden floor.

"That's your man right there." The barman pointed at the new arrival. "Regular as clockwork."

15

———

Leo and Allissa watched the man lumber toward an empty booth in the far corner. He was well over six-feet tall and as wide as two men. His body swayed as though relying on centrifugal force to prevent him from falling over. He reached the booth and slid into the seats.

"I better make Otto his usual. Excuse me." The barman scuttled to the back bar and grabbed one of the bottles of spirits.

"What does he drink?" Leo said, over the guitar solo on whatever soft rock tune was pumping through the speakers. To Leo, they all sounded the same.

"Tequila sunrise," the barman replied. "Well, it's Otto's version of it, anyway. He can't get enough of them."

"Come on. Let's find out what happened last night," Allissa said, climbing from the stool and heading in Otto's direction. Leo followed a step behind.

"Hi there. Otto, isn't it?" Allissa said. "I need your help with something."

Otto turned to face Allissa, the wide-brimmed hat casting his face into shadow.

"We're looking for the guy you were talking with last night. That's his brother-in-law." Allissa pointed at Leo.

"Yeah, who's that?" he said, licking his lips. His voice had a Texan twang.

"A guy called Andy," Leo said. "You were drinking with him in here last night." Leo dug out his phone, found the picture of Andy and showed it to Otto.

Otto's mouth tensed and he nodded again.

The barman scurried across and placed Otto's drink in front of him. Otto nodded, picked up the glass with a hand the size of a frying pan and downed a third of it. He wiped his lips, then considered Allissa and Leo through narrowed eyes. His grizzled face sagged in the dim overhead light.

"Hey, you cops?" Otto barked.

"No," Allissa said. "We're missing persons investigators. We're trying to track down that man."

"If you're sure you're not cops. I ain't done nuthin' to talk to cops about."

"We're definitely not," Allissa said.

"Well, okay." Otto's face cracked into a smile. "Say, if you're not cops, then you have one of these, too." He pointed at the glass. "They're the best."

Leo and Allissa shared a glanced. "Alright," Leo said, going to the bar and making the order. He also ordered Otto a re-fill, thinking the additional booze may loosen him up a bit.

"What y'all wanna know then?" Otto slurred.

"We're looking for this guy." Allissa showed Otto the picture again. "Did you see him last night?"

Otto wrapped a giant hand around his chin and examined the picture.

"Yeah," he said. "He was in here yesterday. We were drinking together."

"Did he come in on his own?" Allissa asked.

"Yeah, he was on his own. Seemed like an alright guy. Why're you looking for him?" Otto's expression darkened. "You don't wanna hurt him?"

"No nothing like that," Allissa said. "He left his wife and son without telling them where he was going. Everyone's very worried about him."

Otto nodded again.

"Did you and Andy leave here together last night?" Allissa asked.

Otto thought for a moment. "Not sure. Can't remember." Otto rubbed his nose, sniffed, and emptied the glass.

"Do you remember what you talked about?" Allissa asked.

Otto looked confused.

"With Andy last night? Do you remember what you spoke about?"

"Just the usual stuff. He was visiting New York. Actually, no, I remember now." Otto pointed at Allissa. "He said that he couldn't remember why he was here. I think he'd had a bit too much of something or other." Otto dabbed his nose.

"He didn't know where he was?" Leo asked.

Otto picked up the empty glass and tried to take a swig from it. Leo doubted these drinks were his first of the day.

"He knew that he was in New York, but he couldn't remember why. He said he was sure he'd figure it out before too long. Sounded crazy, but we get all sorts in this city. He was a good guy. From England. Where're you guys from?"

"We're from England too," Leo said. "Did he seem okay? You know, did he seem injured or hurt or confused?"

Otto chewed over an answer for such a long time that Leo thought he'd probably forgotten the question.

"Was he in a good mood?" Leo asked.

"Yeah, I think so. He was good. He didn't seem injured. Just like a normal guy. Good drinker, too."

The barman delivered the three tequila sunrises. Leo took a sip and felt the alcohol instantly burn the back of this throat.

"Where did you and Andy sit?" Allissa said.

"Right here," Otto replied, poking the table. "This is my seat. I always sit here."

The strong alcohol hit Leo's stomach, and he felt instantly nauseous. Leo glanced up as a group of people banged through the door carrying instruments and speakers. They made a beeline for the small stage and started plugging things in.

"These guys are good," Otto said, pointing a finger at the band. "The Kat Trio. They're here every night, I think."

Leo's eyes panned across the room as another few people wandered in from the street. A group of young women walking away from the bar carrying cocktails that sparkled caught his attention.

"That stuff's all for show," Otto said, pointing at the women. "They're trying to modernize this place. They want all the young people in now. You know, the sort of people who only buy one drink, but take a hundred pictures of it. Makes no sense to me, but that's the way things are now, I s'pose."

As though on cue, a woman in a silver dress removed a smartphone from her bag and snapped a picture of her drink as it billowed thick white smoke.

"There's always famous people in here too," Otto said proudly. "Film stars, singers, all that. That's the kind of place it is. But don't be fooled by them. Most of them got nothing to spend at all."

"I thought the film stars were supposed to be rich," Allissa said, coaxing conversation from the Texan.

"That's what they want you to believe. In truth, they spend so much on their lifestyles, that they have nothing left. It's the people you've never heard of. They're the ones with the most money."

Leo encouraged Otto with a flick of his wrist.

"You see that guy?" Otto pointed toward a guy in the booth next to theirs. "He's the prince of some Middle Eastern country. He spends about three months over here, and when he does, he's in here every night." Otto pointed to another man. "His family owns about a third of the city. You wouldn't recognize them out on the street at all, but I suppose that's the way they like it."

"Do you remember whether you and Andy left here together last night?" Allissa said, pushing the conversation back in a helpful direction. "Anything you can tell us would be so helpful."

"Lady, I had enough of these to pickle a lion. We coulda left at the same time, or he coulda left before. I don't know."

"No problem," Allissa said, climbing to her feet. "Thanks for your help. I think we've taken up enough of your time."

Leo and Allissa shuffled out of the booth and slipped through the crowd toward the bar. Shaded lamps cast a soft glow over the tables, washing the drinkers' faces in a golden hue.

The music playlist faded out and the band started their first song. The crowd's energy increased as people moved to the beat.

"I think it's worth hanging around here a while," Allissa said, propping herself on the bar. "Andy isn't used to big cities like this, so I think there's a good chance he'll come back."

Leo's gaze locked on Allissa, her skin glowing in the soft light. He remembered them running through the street party in St Lucia — although just the day before; it felt like months had passed.

"If he wasn't too drunk to remember where it was," Leo said.

"Good point," Allissa said. "We'll have to wait and see."

Leo dug out his phone. "I'm just going to check on Emma," he said, turning for the door. "You don't mind?"

"Not at all," Allissa said, raising her glass toward the band. "These guys are good. I'll keep a lookout in here, too."

As Leo shoved his way through to the door, Allissa did a full rotation of the bar. Seeing no one who looked a bit like Andy, she turned her attention to the band. Despite the noise of the music, the drinking, and the dancing, the place was comfortable.

An uproar of laughter echoed from a group of men. Allissa glanced at them. They wore crisp shirts and the glazed expression of immature drinkers. She turned to watch the group who'd just arrived greet some friends on the dancefloor before heading to the bar.

"Hey, how are you?"

Allissa assumed the voice wasn't talking to her and continued to watch the crowd. A hand touched her on the arm. She stopped, turned, and stared into the deep grey eyes of the man beside her.

"Are you looking for someone?" the man asked Allissa. Allissa hadn't noticed him before. In his early thirties, he had a wide exuberant smile and a comma of thick brown hair. There was something about him that Allissa recognized, though she couldn't work out what it was.

"Yes, sort of." She took a sip of her drink. "I want to talk to someone about a friend of mine. He was in here last night."

The man's expression didn't change.

"Were you here last night?" Allissa asked.

The man's eyes flicked to the left. Allissa noticed the gesture but didn't understand it. A calm smile broke across his face. His teeth shone iridescent beneath the bar's colorful lights.

"Yes, I was, actually," he said. "I work just around the corner. I often work late and come down to unwind afterward."

"Fantastic," Allissa said, hardly believing her luck. "We're searching for a guy called Andy. If you were here, you might be able to help." She dug out her phone. "We know he was in here, but don't know his movements after that."

"Gotcha. Sure. Anything I can do to help." The man took a swig from a bottle of beer. "You don't sound like you're from around here?" He flashed a sparkling smile at Allissa.

"No, we're missing persons investigators," Allissa said, briefly explaining Andy's disappearance.

"Oh, cool. What a great job. Do you travel a lot?"

"Let me show you a picture of the guy we're looking for." Allissa steered the conversation back to the case and showed him the picture of Andy. "Did you see him in here last night?"

The man leaned in and stared at the photograph for a few seconds. Allissa watched his expression. He showed no signs of recognition.

"I don't think I remember him." He shook his head. "Nothing jumps out, anyway."

"Okay, no problem," Allissa said. "Do you recognize anyone else here now who was also here last night?"

The man gazed around the bar. "I can't see anyone I recognize, but I'll keep looking. Do you want a drink while I'm thinking about it?" He pointed toward Allissa's glass, which was drawing toward empty. "If you're allowed to drink on the job, that is." The shining smile lit up his face again.

"I'm good, thanks," Allissa told him.

"You don't even have to talk to me while you drink it if you don't want to." He got the barman's attention. "What will it be? The same again?"

"No way," Allissa muttered, throwing a glance at Otto. The wide-brimmed hat had sunk even lower over the cowboy's face. "Just a bottle of beer, please."

The man made the order, and a few seconds later, a beer appeared. Allissa took the bottle somewhat reluctantly. Looking at the man, she once again sensed the pang of recognition. She had seen this man before, certainly, although she wasn't sure where.

"I'm sorry I've not introduced myself." The man offered his hand. "My name's Seth Stryker."

Allissa accepted the proffered hand.

"I run a true crime blog," Seth said. "This last week's been pretty crazy with this killer all over the news."

Allissa's eyes narrowed as a realization dawned.

"That's where I recognize you from!" Allissa said, pointing at him. "You were on the news this morning, right?"

"That's right," Seth nodded. "The news stations get me to comment when they have nothing else to go on."

"Does that happen often?" Allissa asked.

"More than you'd think. There are so many news stations with hours to fill. They always want someone to comment on one crime or another."

"How do you know what to say if the police aren't releasing information?" Allissa said.

"They love it when I compare the case to historical crimes. That's what my website's all about. History's greatest criminals and how they get away with it. It's grown out of all proportion really," Seth said. "I didn't start it to get rich or anything. I just wrote about the stuff I found interesting."

"You must have lots of readers."

"Yeah, a few million a year. People are just intrigued, I think. And I thought I was the only one!"

"You must know a lot about what's happening in the city?" Allissa said.

"Yeah, I keep up with the news. There's always something dark and dangerous going on in New York." Seth's phone trilled, and he glanced at it. "I'm sorry, I'm going to have to go."

"Some news?" Allissa said, suddenly interested.

"I'm not sure yet," Seth spoke without looking up from his phone. He typed out a quick reply. Seth looked up and Allissa thought his eyes shone more brightly than before. "Sorry to cut this short. Send me a picture of the guy you're looking for. You never know, I may be able to help you."

Allissa thought about it for a moment and then read out her number. Seth entered it into his phone and vanished into the crowd.

"How's Emma," Allissa said five minutes later when Leo returned. Looking at his face, Allissa realized the question was rhetorical. Emma's pain would be cutting a hole in Leo's heart, too.

"You know, worried sick," Leo said dejectedly. "I wish we could do more. The strange thing is, I get the feeling he's close."

Allissa pulled Leo into a hug.

"You'll never guess who I just met," she said, pulling away a few seconds later.

Leo looked at her blankly. "If I'll never guess, this could take some time. Santa? Meatloaf? Ronaldo?"

"How do you know who Ronaldo is?" Allissa probed. "You know nothing about..."

"I don't. I've just seen the name written on adverts and stuff," Leo admitted.

"As we haven't got the rest of our lives to discuss this, I'll tell you. I just met that guy we saw on the news at Niki's office."

"The serial killer dude?" Leo said.

"Well, the guy who's the expert on serial killers. He runs a true crime blog. The news stations interview him when they have little to go on." Allissa paused to sip her beer. "It's probably best we don't go around calling people serial killers, what with there actually being one on the loose right now."

"Good point," Leo said. "Will he be any help in finding living people too?"

"He was here last night. His office is nearby, so he often stops by after work. He didn't see Andy, though, unfortunately."

Leo's phone beeped. He looked at it quickly, his expression panicked. "It's Niki, she's calling. I'd better answer it."

Leo pushed his way back through the crowd and out on to the street. Leo answered the call and jammed the phone against his ear.

"Leo, a contact of Axel's thinks he's seen Andy," Niki said, not bothering with a greeting. "Washington Square. I'm on my way now, but you may be closer. Get there as soon as you can."

THIS WAY he could see her before he committed. The clothes women wore out in the evening left little to the imagination. He looked around the room and eyed a few women now, paying special attention to what he could see of their figures beneath the tight fitting clothes. Later, he would get to know what was beneath, intimately.

There was more to it than that, though. This way, he could see how she acted with her friends. He could watch her smiling and laughing and then draw her away from the safety of the group.

He glanced across the throng and saw a woman looking back. As his eyes met hers, she glanced the other way. The lingering of her eyes from across the room was enough.

He observed her coolly and lifted the beer to his lips. She was beautiful. A dress of iridescent blue clung to her body. She spun around and he examined her back, the bulge of her bum and the impossible slenderness of her legs.

He turned and ordered another beer.

"Don't you dance?" came a voice from behind him a few minutes later.

Even before turning, he knew who it was. He inhaled and pictured her — the shimmering dress, the cascading long hair, and the gleaming smile.

He took a sip from the bottle and turned. The temperature in the room had risen and a humid haze now hung in the air.

"I prefer to watch. You're all doing such a good job that..." He let his voice trail off.

She considered him and then offered him a hand. He accepted it, introduced himself, and kissed her on the cheek.

Taking a sharp breath, he inhaled the scent of her skin. She smelled good, very good indeed.

"If you don't dance, what do you come here for?"

A good question, he thought.

"You know, to unwind after the day. Do you want a drink, by the way?" He raised his beer.

"Sure." She selected something from the menu.

He smirked at the cost. Well, okay, he thought, as it's your last.

16

"Washington Square. Quick as you can," Allissa shouted, jumping into the back of a taxi. The rain had increased while they were inside and now slammed against the asphalt like angry fists.

The taxi swished through the wet streets at an annoyingly sedate pace.

"How sure did Niki sound?" Allissa said, glancing at him again.

"She didn't say, exactly." Leo watched a solitary figure walk a dog into a side street. "She left a photo of Andy with Axel, remember? He must have somehow circulated it to people he knows. One of them got in touch to say they'd seen someone matching Andy's description. It could be nothing."

"Let's hope it's not," Allissa said, glancing through the window as they powered across an intersection. The lights of the city reflected in the wet street, creating a kaleidoscope of color. Neon signs flickered, and storefront windows cast a warm glow onto the sidewalk.

"I wonder how Axel got the word out," Leo said. "He

can't have half of New York's homeless population traipsing through his bedroom daily."

"Carrier pigeon, maybe," Allissa quipped.

"I wouldn't be surprised," Leo replied, deadpan. "But so far, that guy's intel has got results. Although I'll admit I have no idea how."

"*Intel, that gets results*," Allissa repeated, mocking Leo's voice. "Have you joined the CIA or something?"

Despite the late hour, life continued to throng through the streets of the city. People wandered from one place to the next or huddled outside bars and clubs, smoking, and chatting beneath umbrellas.

Ten minutes later, the cab skidded to the side of the road. Allissa pushed a fifty-dollar bill through the plastic divider and then they piled out of the car.

"Washington Square is just over there," Allissa shouted, pointing at the dark outline of a park on the opposite side of an intersection.

They charged straight across the road and then paused, looking amid the gloomy trees. Washington Square Arch glowed from one side of the park, although the rest of the space was lit only by the occasional dim streetlight.

A scream sliced through the muted sounds of the city. The sound rooted Leo to the spot. Leo's head whipped from side to side, his heart rate spiking as the scream echoed in his ears.

"What was that?" Allissa said, also searching the gloomy scene ahead.

Leo reached out and grabbed Allissa's arm in a protective hold. His eyes scanned the dark expanse of the park, searching for any sign of movement. He saw nothing.

The scream came again, followed by the sound of a scuffle. The scream resonated uselessly from the rain-soaked trees and ornate stone arch, then faded to silence.

"It's coming from in there," Allissa said, pointing between the trees.

Without a second thought, Leo and Allissa charged straight into the park. They ran down a pitch-black pathway, heading toward the scream. Here and there, sporadic streetlights punctuated the pervasive darkness, creating pools of illumination amid the enveloping shadows.

Another shriek filled the night air, this time muted as though a hand was forced across the screecher's mouth.

Leo sped up, his feet slipping across the wet path. For a split second, he wondered whether they were doing the right thing, running toward the scream. As they ran further into the park, the sound of movement reverberated from somewhere nearby.

"Stop!" Leo shouted, sounding a lot braver than he felt. "We've called the police. They'll be here in a minute." Leo pulled them to a stop and spun from side to side. He took a second to listen carefully, attempting to tune in to any movement.

"This way," Allissa shouted, dragging them to the left. "Someone's moving down there."

They skirted an area of grass and bare flower beds, their feet thundering over the wet cobbles.

Then, sending another spear of ice through Leo's spine, another muted cry echoed through the park.

Leo and Allissa swung around a corner and saw a figure, or maybe two figures, locked together. Still thirty feet away, shrouded by total blackness, all Leo could make out was a writhing shape in the gloom. The figures struggled one way, sliding across the ground, and then writhed back the way they'd come.

"Stop!" Leo shouted again. "The police are on their way!"

Leo broke away from Allissa and charged on. For the first few footsteps, Leo couldn't make out what was going on. Then he saw metal reflecting some far away light. He knew instantly what he was looking at — a blade.

Sirens wailed from the street behind them. Echoing frantically from the surrounding buildings, it wasn't clear where the sirens came from, although Leo hoped they were heading in their direction. Clearly, Leo and Allissa hadn't been the only people to hear the screaming, as someone had called the police.

Leo hurtled on toward the knife-holder, his footsteps almost soundless on the rain-soaked grass. He covered the distance in a few seconds and smashed his full weight against the figure's back. The attacker, which Leo could now tell was a man, groaned and stumbled forward. Leo clung on as the man's feet scrambled for grip. The man found his footing and turned, grunting and groaning. The knife glimmered menacingly and then zipped through the air.

Leo pushed harder, trying to shove the man off balance. He glanced down and saw a woman drag herself away. It looked as though her clothes were crumpled and torn, but from what Leo could tell she was unharmed. The woman whimpered and crawled, clearly still too shaken to climb to her feet.

In his peripheral vision, Leo saw the knife swing in his direction. He twisted to the left, avoiding the blade with half an inch to spare. He spun around and elbowed the assailant in the face. The man let out a grunt as the strike connected, his groan quickly morphing into a snarl of rage.

One hundred feet away — close, but still too far to help — several police cruisers squealed to a stop. Their strobing light bars flickered amid the trees.

Momentarily distracted by his diminishing options, the attacker spun around and fled.

With a quick look back, Leo confirmed Allissa, and the victim were out of immediate danger. The beams of flashlights danced somewhere back there now too, as police officers swarmed into the park. Leo could also hear voices, although they were muted over the roar of the adrenaline in his ears.

As the attacker broke into a sprint, Leo acted on pure instinct. He lunged forward, aiming to tackle the man to the ground. His hands reached out but grabbed nothing but air.

Sensing the movement, the attacker glanced over his shoulder. He tried to quicken his pace, but his shoes slipped on the wet grass.

Leo charged forward again, closing in on the fleeing figure.

The man spun around and went on the offensive once again. He swung the knife high, the blade glimmering in the scant light. The blade arched through the air.

Leo swung his arm up and grabbed the hand which held the knife. His fingers wrapped around the man's wrist as he struggled with all the force he could muster, attempting to push the blade away.

Leo's feet skidded across the wet grass, and he almost lost his balance. His heart pounded, each throb a drumbeat that echoed a single thought — keep that blade as far away as possible.

Leo twisted the wrist, trying to control the weapon. He gritted his teeth and used all his strength to loop an elbow around the man's right hand. He attempted to pull the arm back, but the man was powerful. The blade shuddered as both men struggled for control. The arm, and blade remained still, locked in midair.

Then, the assailant spun with unexpected agility and sent a fist into Leo's stomach. Air whooshed from his lungs in a painful hiss and Leo doubled over. The attacker shoved Leo away, brandished the knife once again and closed in.

Just twenty feet away, flashlight beams whipped through the park as officers ran toward the scene on foot.

"Over here!" Allissa shouted. "Get over here now!"

In one swift movement, the attacker lunged forward, the knife outstretched. Leo rolled over, pulling himself across the earth. The move sent the blade wide, but not far enough.

The pain was immediate and intense. A white-hot line seared across Leo's shoulder. His knees and arms buckled, and he collapsed to the ground, gasping for breath. His vision lost focus and the shapes of dark, and light spun around him.

17

LEO SPRAWLED BACK on the grass as lights whipped above him, illuminating the falling rain as though freezing it in time. He rolled over as best he could and saw the attacker sprinting away through the trees. Even with his shoulder screaming in pain, Leo tried to remember all he could about the man. He was lean, slightly over six feet, light, and surprisingly strong. When the figure merged completely into the darkness, Leo rolled on to his back. His head hit the earth, and he felt the vibrations of feet running — somehow, he got the impression that some were running toward him while others were running away.

"You've been hurt!" Allissa said, her voice laced with panic. She raced across to Leo and held his shoulders. "What happened?"

"He was too quick," Leo hissed. "I tried to move, but he was too quick."

Leo felt something warm ooze across his shoulder but couldn't work out what it was. Shouting voices rolled toward him, and Leo attempted to prop himself up on his elbows.

Pain seared through his shoulder, and he shouted, dropping back to the ground.

"Don't move," Allissa said, scooting around so that she was sitting beside his head. She assessed his injuries as best she could in the gloom.

"Over here!" Allissa shouted, waving her arms to attract the approaching officers. Four officers rounded the corner, and hearing Allissa's cries, charged in their direction, flashlight beams thrashing around.

"How's the victim?" Leo asked, trying to look toward where Allissa had pulled the young woman out of harm's way.

Two beams converged on Leo, dazzling him. The beams hovered for a second and then moved off and focused on something behind him. Leo wanted to turn and see what they were looking at behind him, but his body felt weak.

"She's fine. No physical injuries. I think we interrupted him just in time," Allissa said. She looked across at the woman, who was now looked after by an officer. "I don't think she will get much sleep tonight, though."

The officers covered the ground quickly. One paused to assess Leo's condition. Allissa froze as the light passed across Leo's shoulder. Leo glanced down and saw a gash across his shoulder, blood seeping from his shirt. He winced at the sight of the injury, then tensed, attempting not to cry out.

"Stop where you are!" another officer shouted. Leo thought about pointing out that he was hardly in danger of running away but felt too weak to even speak. Then he noticed the officer focusing on something off in the distance.

"Hang in there. You're going to be fine," an officer said, glancing down at Leo and Allissa. "Medics are on the way."

The officer pulled out his radio and called for medical help. Leo found the man's calm and professional tone somewhat reassuring.

"I'm fine, I'm fine!" Leo hissed. "Don't worry about me. He went that way." Leo pointed in the direction the assailant had fled. "He can't have gone far."

Two officers wasted no time in setting off after the attacker, their flashlights piercing the darkness ahead. One officer crouched beside Leo and pulled out a small medical kit. He applied pressure to the wound with a balled-up bandage. "The wound isn't as big as it looks," the officer said. "But we need to keep pressure on to slow the bleeding. Stay calm, you'll be fine."

Allissa scooted around to allow the officer to work and took Leo's hand. He felt cold, lying exposed in the park.

A hundred feet away, beams bounced from the trees and shrubs as the officers ran through the park in pursuit of the killer. Fleeting shadows whipped from side to side, exaggerating the officer's movements.

The cry of another siren pierced the night.

"That's the medics now," the officer said, glancing over his shoulder. "They will be here in less than a minute."

"Stop! We have you surrounded!" shouted a police officer.

"You hear that 'action man'?" Allissa said, squeezing Leo's hand. "They've got him. I think you might just be a hero."

Leo smiled weakly. "It's not all it's cracked up to be," Leo said, exhaling. "I wish I'd had that drink now."

"Freeze, put your hands up!" a voice boomed from the officers, they were moving in on the suspect.

"Niki is going to be really impressed that you stopped a serial killer," Allissa said, her hand still clutching Leo's.

"Jealous, more like," Leo muttered, focusing on the warmth of Allissa's hand. He enjoyed the feeling of her so close and hoped that she wouldn't move.

"We've got him!" another of the officers said. "Suspect secure."

A third voice grumbled from the gloom, although what it said was intelligible.

"His personal effects are all over the ground here. Pick them up." One officer directed the other. "Bringing him over now."

The rustling of foliage and a cacophony of grunts and groans followed, marking the struggle as the officers moved the suspect. The flashlights once again swept through the shrubbery, toward Leo and Allissa.

The scene was soon bolstered by the additional officers and medics from the road behind. Their flashlights cut through the darkness, painting the wet park in swaths of light and shadow. The chatter of their radios hissed into the air.

The silhouetted man, now handcuffed, and under control, appeared from gloom. With an officer on either side, they marched him back toward Leo and Allissa. The man struggled, but his resistance was futile against the officer's firm grip.

The officers and the suspect rounded a few shrubs, and Leo saw the man's outline in more detail.

He struggled up to get a better look. He knew instantly that something was wrong. The man who attacked Leo had been tall and athletic, this man was wider bodied and staggered with the telltale signs of a drunk.

As the beams of the flashlights passed over the man's face, throwing the man's features into sharp relief. Leo gasped and for a second, all his pain was forgotten.

"It can't be," Allissa said, seeing the man at the same time as Leo.

"It's not possible," Leo muttered, straining to keep his eyes locked on the suspect's face.

Leo knew, that wasn't the face of a killer. That was a face he'd seen countless times before.

"Andy!" Allissa shouted.

18

LEO COULDN'T PINPOINT where or when his dislike for hospitals had begun. Although there wasn't a particular event that had put him off, every time he found himself in one, whether as a patient or a visitor, the walls closed in around him.

Maybe it was the relentless flicker of fluorescent lights overhead, the pervasive scent of antiseptic that dominated the air, or the muffled conversations that drifted over the curtain dividers—each sounding as though it was a discussion of life and death.

Whatever the cause, as Leo sat there, the grip of anxiety tightened around his chest.

"I hear you've saved our city from a serial killer," the nurse said, her tone light as she focused on the task at hand. With gentle yet expert hands, she dabbed the wound with gauze to remove the blood and carefully examined the extent of the injury.

"It was nothing, really," Leo said, trying not to wince as the pain shot through his body.

"Modest too," the nurse replied.

"He's always like that," Allissa said, sitting on a chair by the door. "This guy wouldn't know how to take a compliment if it came with instructions."

"I know the type," the nurse giggled. "Most of the men I treat, are either as modest as a saint," she pointed at Leo, "or think they're God's gift to the world."

The women laughed, but Leo remained silent.

"It could have been a lot worse," Allissa said, pacing across the room to get a good look at the injury. Leo had no idea how she could even bear to look at it. Just the thought of blood made his stomach turn.

"The good news is that it's shallow. In fact, we don't even need stitches."

"What!" Allissa said. "You mean all this fuss and it's just a scratch?" Allissa pointed mockingly at Leo.

"It's still a serious injury," the nurse said. "Nothing like this should be taken lightly."

"I'm not. I'm just glad for all our sakes you don't need stitches. This guy can take on a serial killer, but when it comes to needles." She shivered animatedly.

"You'll have to knock me out," Leo muttered, Allissa's mood lightening his anxiety.

"This might sting a little," the nurse said, applying a generous amount of antibiotic ointment. Then, with precise movements, she placed a sterile, bandage over the wound.

"That wasn't too bad, was it?" the nurse said.

"Which bit? Being stabbed by a serial killer, or the treatment?" Leo said.

With the wound dressed, the nurse wrapped Leo's shoulder in a bandage, pulling it taut enough to hold the dressing in place and support the injured area without restricting circulation.

"This should keep it secure," she said, fastening the end

of the bandage. "Monitor the wound for any signs of infection — redness or swelling. If you see anything concerning, come straight back."

"Thank you," Leo said, slipping his shirt back on again and wincing at each movement. He struggled up on to his feet.

"And take it easy, okay? It will heal fastest without too much movement. No more wrestling in the park with killers."

"I'll make sure of that," Allissa said, flashing Leo a glance. "You're staying on the sofa for a week."

"Make it two," the nurse added.

Leo smiled half-heartedly, his mind still on the events of the night. The rain, the chase, and the face of the man who wasn't his attacker after all played on a loop through his mind's eye.

Allissa opened the door, and the pair stepped out into the corridor.

"I need to get some air," Leo said, wandering toward the elevators. He waited for a pair of nurses to enter, their coats pulled tightly around blue uniforms, and then followed them inside.

Three minutes later, Leo and Allissa stepped out into the early morning air. The sky had lightened whilst they'd been inside, and now glowed with the pink and purple of a new day. Leo took a long and slow breath. The cold, fresh air slid deep into his lungs.

He padded slowly away from the entrance and slumped onto a bench, moving just an inch at a time to trying to prevent the bandage rubbing against the wound.

The rain which had sloshed through the city overnight had retreated and left the sky clear. It wasn't cold to Leo, though, it was revitalizing.

"What're you thinking about?" The bench creaked as Allissa sat down beside Leo. "Silly question, really, sorry."

Leo turned toward Allissa. The morning light softened her features. Her billowing breath mingled with his in the space between them.

"What was I thinking?" Leo asked.

Allissa wrapped her arms around herself and suppressed a shiver.

"I was thinking about you, actually," Leo said, staring deep into Allissa's eyes. The surrounding noise evaporated. Allissa smiled. She put her hand on top of Leo's on the bench. Leo glanced down at their hands. Her touch warmed his skin. "Last night, taking that guy on…"

"That was really heroic, by the way," Allissa said. "Even I was impressed, and I am kinda hard to please."

"Thanks," Leo replied, weakly. "But it's because of you, I think."

"What do you mean?"

"I never really had a reason to do stuff like that. I would run the other way at the first sign of trouble, but things are different now."

"They certainly are…"

The pair sat in silence for a moment.

"Andy isn't the killer," Leo said, looking down at his hands. "There's no way."

"That's not what the police are saying." Allissa sighed, letting out a breath that felt as though it held the weight of the world. "They say the first murder happened the night he went missing."

"But he was blind drunk. So drunk that he drove the car into the wall of a tunnel." Leo's muscles tensed, then he forced himself to relax.

"I know." Allissa's hand snaked across the bench and

covered his. "I feel as though we've just landed ourselves even more work to do."

"Yes, but now the stakes are even higher," Leo said, sitting forward. Through the pain and fatigue, a sense of purpose rose.

"And the killer is still out there," Allissa said, watching a man and a woman run together down the street. The woman strode out in front with her black hair swaying. Their colorful clothes shone in the early light.

"We need to see this through," Leo muttered.

"But you're on desk duty." Allissa turned to face him. "You heard what the nurse said. No more wrestling with killers."

"I really don't plan to, but some things..."

"Hold on," Allissa interrupted. "Here comes the cavalry."

Michael and Nadia rounded the corner and strode toward Leo and Allissa. Emma walked dejectedly a few steps behind, clutching Frankie by the hand. And behind Emma and Frankie, walked Niki. The small group reached Leo and Alissa and fanned out as though ogling at wild animals in the zoo.

Allissa had already communicated the news with them all. She now gave them an update on Leo's injury, including the details about him almost losing consciousness at the sight of his own blood just hours after facing down a serial killer. Emma, Michael, and Nadia remained emotionless, but Niki flashed her lopsided grin.

"How can Andy have done this?" Emma said, pacing backward and forward. "He was only away for a few hours, and he's killed three women, and attempted a fourth." Emma froze and swung around to face Leo. "And tried to kill you."

Leo locked eyes with his sister. She was deathly pale; her

skin's only color were the black marks which bracketed her eyes.

"He didn't," Leo said. Although he spoke quietly, his words were hard edged. "The killer in the park last night wasn't Andy. He was taller and slimmer. I'd have recognized Andy for sure."

"You told this to the police?" Emma snapped.

"Of course he did," Allissa replied. "He told them many times. They say that it was dark, and Leo was confused and didn't remember correctly."

"Are they charging Andy for the murders?" Michael said, his voice grave.

"That's the way it looks," Niki said. "The night he went missing was the night of the first murder. The timeline is tight, but it's possible."

"But he didn't," Emma said, now. "He couldn't have done this!"

"I know," Leo said, unable to look his sister in the eye. As well as the physical pain, and the mental exhaustion, guilt now sat heavily on his chest. Whilst they had successfully found Andy, they had also led the police directly to him. Andy was now far worse off for Leo's intervention.

Allissa grabbed Leo's chin and turned him to face her. "Whatever you're thinking, stop it," she said, successfully reading his thoughts. "This is not our fault. We will sort this out, right?" Allissa looked up at Niki.

"We sure will," Niki said. "And you know the best way to do that?"

Within his chest, Leo's heart locked on a course of action. He looked up at the surrounding people, his gaze lingering on his sister for longer than the others. Finally, he looked at Niki. "We need to find the real killer."

19

THEY SAY that your entire life cascades through your mind just before death — or so Andy had been told. Those last fleeting seconds are said to be a window for reflecting on your life's choices and the risks you've embraced. They give you the opportunity, in total freedom, to find peace with your worldly shortcomings and discover something positive, happy, and fulfilling.

That probably would have happened to Andy as the car careened through the tunnel if he hadn't been so drunk. He'd been drinking all day. There were the beers at the airport, then on the plane, then the crate he'd bought at the shop. Finally, he'd ended the night with a bottle of whiskey. Considering that, as the Porsche spun through the tunnel at eighty miles per hour, all Andy could think about were the events of the last few hours. But it didn't really matter. He couldn't remember it, anyway.

Andy opened his eyes and light tore into his retinas.

"Turn off the lights, will you?" he muttered. His voice was croaky and weak. It didn't sound like him at all.

The lights continued to blaze. Andy swore and strained

his eyes closed again. Colors danced across his eyelids. His head throbbed.

Usually, vague memories joined the dancing colors. Andy lay still and tried to think. No memories came forth. His mind remained blank. That was unusual.

He rubbed his face with the palms of his hands. His skin felt rough and dusty.

A glass of water, a strong coffee, and some headache pills — that's what he needed now.

"Emma, you there?" Andy shouted.

He would down the pills, give them a few minutes to kick in, and then he'd be able to open his eyes and work out what day it was.

He didn't have work, did he? Andy felt a sudden stab of confusion. No, he was sure he didn't have to go to work. Although he liked to drink, Andy didn't think he would have got in a state like this on a work night.

"Emma!" Andy shouted again.

Then Andy heard a voice reply. It wasn't Emma's.

"Who you callin' Emma?" came the reply in a voice that certainly wasn't Emma's. The voice was deep, male, and if Andy could hear correctly, American.

Andy pushed himself upright and opened his eyes. The light seared a hole straight into his brain. Andy jammed his eyes closed and rested back on his elbows. Every inch of his body ached. There was something seriously wrong with this bed. He just couldn't get comfortable.

"I'm talkin' to you, boy," the man said again. "Who you callin' Emma?"

Andy drew a deep breath. He'd heard of people hearing voices, but he'd never known that on a hangover. Maybe this was a sign that he should stop drinking so much.

"First you shoutin' all night, now you're ignoring me, boy. Well, that ain't happening."

A pair of thick hands pulled Andy to his feet. Andy's brain pounded, as though the movement sent it sloshing against the sides of his skull. Every muscle ached.

"Hey, what, you can't... wait..." Andy struggled to form words. He opened his eyes and tried to look around. The light stung and his brain thumped.

"Na, you've been here all night, boy, snoring like a train and shouting for Emma. None of us got a wink of sleep."

Andy turned toward the voice's owner. He squinted and his eyes finally focused.

A tall and heavily muscled man held him by the arm. Andy struggled to keep upright. The man dragged Andy forward. A fresh wave of pain rattled through Andy's body.

"Where am I? What... who..."

Andy glanced around again. His eyes felt as though they'd dried against the walls of his skull, but his vision had now improved enough for him to see.

Andy did a three-sixty of the room. Gray walls surrounded him on all sides, punctuated with the occasional scratch of faded graffiti. The only feature in the room was a thick metal door, which was currently closed.

"Where am I?" Andy muttered, his voice a murmur.

The man swung around and glanced at two men sitting on beds behind him. Andy noticed the other men for the first time. They were all large, bulging with muscles and covered in tattoos. The thugs all roared with laughter. They eyed each other and then looked at Andy as though he were a lamb that had just wandered into a lion's den. The two men at the back stood up, causing the metal beds to screech.

Andy glanced at the stainless-steel toilet and sink combo

in the corner. He swallowed hard, but his throat already felt as though it had sealed itself closed.

"Dorothy has left Kansas, that's for sure," the first man said, pulling Andy closer. Andy's stomach flitted at the smell of the other man's sweat.

"Let me tell you, this is not the sort of place you wanna be spendin' too much time." The man glanced sideways at the other two, who now surrounded Andy like a wall of human muscle and bone. "What do you think? Should we give him the welcome tour?"

"Definitely," the man to the right said.

"Wait, wait! No" Andy tried to move but could barely struggle beneath the vice-like grip. Andy pulled a deep breath. The air tasted like disinfectant and sweat. "I don't know what's going on here, but there must be some explanation."

"Yeah. I got an explanation," the leading thug said. "You've been put in here so that we can teach you a lesson." The man lifted Andy clean off the ground by the throat. Andy grabbed at the man's hands, but the other thugs pulled his arms away. For a moment, it felt as though his arms would be pulled clean from his body.

"There's an important lesson you need to learn," the thug said, drawing his face in close to Andy's. "Are you listening?"

Andy tried to nod, but his neck could hardly move.

"I can't hear you. Is that yes?" The thug said.

Andy tried to speak, but his voice just came out as a gurgle. The thug released his hold for a second.

"Yes, I'm listening," Andy said, before sucking in another deep breath.

"Good. Everyone in here is a criminal," the thug said.

"Isn't that, right?" he glanced at the man-mountain either side and both men grumbled their agreement.

"On the outside, where you're used to living, it's easy to think that all criminals are the same. But that's not the case."

"Not the case at all," one man echoed.

"Coz, in here you got good criminals, like us," the man nodded at the thugs on either side of him.

"We're the good kind of criminals, yeah," one man grunted in reply.

"We might do a bit of dealing, a bit of robbery, maybe fraud, or something like that," the leader continued. "But what we certainly don't do is go around killing innocent people."

"Especially women," one man added.

"That's right. We don't like criminals killing innocent people. You bring us all a bad name."

"Wait!" Andy groaned, his voice coming out as little more than a hiss.

"I think he's trying to say something," one thug said.

The leader released his hold on Andy's neck.

"I haven't done anything, I don't know what you're talking about," Andy gurgled, his reply, his voice half an octave higher than usual.

The three men laughed, their voices booming from the bare walls.

"We've got a denier!" one man shouted.

"That's funny coz everyone denies it to start with. It takes time for you to realize that denying what you've done slows the entire process down," the leader said. "It's better for everyone if you just tell us how it is."

"It's not... I didn't... I haven't..." Andy stuttered before the hands closed around his neck again.

"That's not what we've heard," the leader said. "We

heard that you've been out there killing innocent women like it's a game."

"No!" Andy groaned!

"You want to deny it? That's okay," the man said, shaking Andy like a rag doll. "But you've been warned." The man nodded at his crew and two more meaty hands grabbed at Andy. "In truth, we like it when people try to deny what they've done."

The two onlooking giggled.

"That means we get to soften you up a little bit, just to make sure you're ready to admit it when the detectives have time to talk to you." The man's hands closed around Andy's throat. "We're saving everyone time, you see."

A deep clanging noise echoed through the cell and the door screeched open. A large officer assessed the scene through narrowed eyes and grinned. "I'm glad you boys are getting on well," he said. "I'm sorry to break up the party, but this little guy's got a visitor."

The man dropped Andy to the floor and stepped away. Andy looked up, wheezing and puffing. He clawed at his throat, trying to breathe.

"Don't worry, he'll be back soon, and you can carry on getting to know each other." The officer forced Andy to his feet and dragged him down a featureless corridor. He unlocked the door and shoved Andy inside.

"Sit there and put your hands on the table." The officer pointed to a metal chair sat beside a table.

Andy did what he was told. The officer leant over and shackled Andy's wrists to a ring in the center of the table. Then, the officer stood, wandered from the room, and shut the door.

20

ANDY SAT in the room for several minutes. His heart thumped as though it was trying to break out of his chest and run away. His body ached all over, and the pain between his eyes getting worse by the minute. Andy rolled his shoulders, attempting to relieve some of the pain in his upper back. The handcuffs drew tight, stopping his movement halfway through.

His pulse finally slowing, Andy turned his attention to the room in which he was currently imprisoned. The place was exactly like one of the stark interview rooms used on all the cop shows he'd seen. The walls were a stained gray color, which seemed to give the space a claustrophobic feel. A single bulb buzzed overhead, casting a harsh glow over the utilitarian table and the two chairs which faced him from the other side.

Andy leaned back, trying but failing to find a more comfortable position in the metal chair. He glanced at himself in the reflection of a large mirror on the wall. His eyes were dark and bloodshot, and his skin looked gray.

A clinking of keys from outside the door drew Andy's

attention. A key crunched in the lock and the door swung open.

"About time. I need to get out of here!" Andy shouted, ready to give the officer a hard time. Then, recognizing the man who stepped through the door, he reeled backward.

"Leo," Andy said, his eyes flaring and his hands dropping to the table. Allissa and Niki followed. Allissa took the seat beside Leo, and Niki leaned against the wall.

"What's... what's going on? What are you doing here?" Andy said. His head whipped from side to side as though trying to take the whole scene in.

The door slammed shut and the key once again turned in the lock.

For almost a minute, Leo didn't reply. All eyes bored into Andy, giving him nowhere to look that wasn't a cold and interrogative stare.

"I don't know what's happened," Andy said. "You've got to help. You've got to get me out of here. There are some guys. They were going to kill me." Andy tried to move, but the shackles binding him to the table clinked and then held.

Leo let out a breath and placed his hands on the table. "How do you feel?" Leo said finally. Andy looked straight ahead and the two men locked eyes.

"I... I... don't know. Where am I? What's going on?" Again, Andy tried to move, but the shackles wouldn't allow it.

"You've been arrested and charged with murder," Allissa said.

All the expression dropped from Andy's face. His features froze, petrified, as the color drained away, leaving a pallor that spoke of the fear gripping his heart. His jaw hung loose, and then he snapped it closed.

"What do you mean? I don't understand?" Andy said, finally.

In simple terms and with no emotion, Allissa explained the events of the last two days. Andy listened in silent shock, his body physically sagging into the chair. Despite the chill in the room, a cold sweat appeared on his forehead. His breathing became just a series of shallow gasps.

"I didn't do it. I didn't do anything," Andy said.

"How do you know that?" Leo said, his voice cold.

Andy stuttered a reply but didn't vocalize it.

"You don't know for certain that you didn't do anything, do you?" Leo said, folding his arms. He winced as a spear of pain shot through him at the movement. He tensed his face, not wanting Andy to see the pain. "You can't know that for certain because you were out of your head drunk."

Andy stuttered another reply and then looked down at the table.

"I know it wasn't you," Leo said, finally putting Andy out of his misery. "The killer tried to stab me. Although it was dark and I couldn't see clearly, I know it wasn't you."

Andy's shoulders sagged with relief.

"That's not enough to get you off, though," Niki said, speaking for the first time. She explained how the investigators had discounted Leo's testimony because he couldn't give them a clear description.

"The question is," Leo said, looking down at Andy's shackled hands and then meeting his brother-in-law's gaze. "Why should we help you?"

"Because... what... I don't understand," Andy said.

"You don't seem to understand very much," Leo said. "Let me make this very clear for you. My sister, your wife, hasn't stopped crying in two days because of what you've done."

"Emma," Andy said, his expression melting. "Is she okay?"

"Not really," Leo said, not even blinking so that he could stare even more intensely at Andy. "To be honest, I think that right now she's better off without you. We could walk out of here now, take Emma and Frankie home, and leave you to deal with this yourself."

Andy squirmed beneath Leo's unrelenting stare. His mouth opened and closed again, and a rivulet of sweat ran down his cheek.

"You could have died in that car," Leo said, "or killed someone else. Then you'd never see your son again."

"Frankie." Andy's eyes shot to Leo's.

"He's doing fine. Missing his dad, though."

Andy inhaled. Tears sparkled.

Leo watched him impassively.

Andy was no longer the man who terrorized Leo about his lifestyle decisions, treated his wife as a servant, or disrespected the generosity of her parents.

"I don't know," Andy said, finally.

"You don't know what?"

"I don't know what happened. I don't know what to do." Andy was becoming more upset now. "I don't know how to be Frankie's dad."

Leo watched the man droop further into the opposite seat. All boastfulness and arrogance seemed to have melted away, leaving just a vulnerable shell of a man.

"You're all new to it, being a dad," Leo said, his voice softening. "You just need to do what you think is right for your son. You're allowed to make mistakes —"

"But I —"

"But first," Leo cut in. He raised a finger to point at Andy and instantly regretted the movement. "First, to even be there for your family, you need to be sober."

Andy stared at Leo. Leo thought for a moment that Andy was going to argue, but he didn't. The Andy of a few days ago would have argued for sure. He would have taken Leo's words as an insult and fought against them tooth and nail. Now, though, the beaten man that he was, just stared at his hands without a word.

"I'm not sure Emma will even want me back now," Andy said, his voice a whisper.

"I don't know either," Leo said. "It wouldn't be surprising if she didn't. She spends all her time with a child who doesn't speak yet. Then you come home in a foul mood and just start drinking."

"But I... I need to work," he said. "We need the money."

"We both know Emma's offered to go back to work instead. She loved her job, and it paid better than yours. Then you could get to know your son."

"But that's not what a dad does," Andy said with failing conviction.

"If a dad is someone who drinks too much, then Frankie doesn't need one," Leo said. "He can just as well do without that."

Andy nodded morosely.

"I'm not telling you what's best," Leo said. "I am telling you to talk to your wife, discuss it, and be open to it. Together, you'll make a definition of being that boy's father that works for you all."

Leo let the comment sit for a minute.

Finally, Andy nodded. All occupants of the room exhaled.

"Then let's get to work," Leo said.

"We know you didn't kill those women, which means the

actual killer is still out there," Niki said, straightening up. "While the police are busy trying to find evidence against you, we are going to find who really did this. To do that, we need to know if you saw anything. You were just fifty feet from the killer."

Andy thought hard for almost two minutes and then shrugged. "I'm sorry, I can't remember anything. The last few days are a total haze. The first thing I remember clearly is the police waking me up. I must have just been sleeping on the ground in the park. No idea why I was there."

Leo sighed. "That's not going to help us very much."

"I'm sorry," Andy said, his head slumping forward "I remember an officer grabbing me. They rolled me over and cuffed my hands. While they did that, all the stuff fell out of my pockets. I only remember that because they spent a while collecting it all up."

"They will have looked through it all for evidence," Niki said.

Andy's face suddenly paled even further. "Michael's watch. I think I took Michael's watch."

"Yes, you did," Allissa commented. "He didn't seem that worried. He's just pleased to hear that you're alright."

"They took it off me when we came here, I remember that. Can you collect it today and give it back to Michael as soon as you can? At least that's one thing I can put right now," Andy said. He placed his hands on the desk and the chains jangled.

"Of course," Leo said, forcing himself to stand. He crossed the room and banged on the door. A key turned and the officer standing outside opened the door. Emma stood in the corridor, the fluorescent lights stripping the last bit of color from her skin.

Emma locked eyes with her husband and then stepped inside the room.

"We will get to work," Leo said, looking from Emma to Andy and back again. "I'll be in touch when there's progress."

WAKING UP, he was tangled in the covers and soaked with sweat. He forced himself out of bed. He'd fallen asleep with the heater on, and the apartment was sweltering. He climbed out of bed and flicked off the ancient electric radiator, then peered at the crack of morning light seeping through the dirty curtains.

Then, like a train out of control, memories of the night before came back to him. He hated that someone had prevented his masterpiece. That was not the way it was supposed to go.

He spun around and examined the dingy apartment, cursing himself for spending the night here. This place should be kept sterile, but realizing the police were not far behind, he had panicked and fled. Still, he shouldn't have stayed here.

He moved the curtain aside an inch and peered through.

The rain had worn itself out, and the morning was bright and cold. Noticing the puddles that still flanked the road, he realized that the rain was a stroke of luck. A storm like that would wash away fingerprints or DNA. Any trace that he had been there at all would now have been destroyed.

Instinctively, he wrapped his right hand around his left wrist. His fingers snaked up and down his damp skin, expecting to feel the bracelet. When his fingers touched nothing but skin, his stomach tensed.

He lifted his arm and stared at his wrist. The bracelet was gone. In a fury, he tore the sheets from the bed, then yanked the bed away from the wall. The bracelet was nowhere in the room. He clenched his fists and thumped them against the wall.

He turned to the sepia-toned photograph hanging above the bed. In the picture, his great-grandfather sat upright, his head tilted backward, looking away to the left of the camera. The man held a domed hat between his hands and a row of military insignia — fakes, as his great-grandfather had never served in the military — glowed proudly from his chest.

"A great man," he whispered to the photograph. "And I will do you proud. You will see. You will see."

21

BACK IN NIKI'S OFFICE, Leo paced across to the window and peered out at the street. Rain pounded against the glass, distorting his view of the street below.

"How long have you guys known each other?" Niki asked, moving across the room. She turned her attention to the documents spread out across the table.

"About two years," Leo replied. He spun around to face Niki, the movement sending a bolt of pain through him.

Having not eaten since the previous evening, Allissa had gone to fetch food from a nearby take-out shop.

"How'd you meet?" Niki asked, glancing up at Leo.

"It was a case, actually," Leo said. He crossed the room and settled into the sofa.

"Let me guess, she was your first client?"

"Something like that," Leo admitted, once again impressed with Niki's ability to read between the lines. "Her dad hired me to find her. It turned out she'd set up a non-profit in Kathmandu, Nepal, to help victims of people traffickers."

"You clearly did a good job," Niki said, looking hard at Leo.

Leo shrugged nonchalantly and then regretted the movement. "It was mostly just good fortune. You know, being in the right place at the right time."

"I don't believe that for a second." Niki folded her arms and stared hard at Leo. "You're both very competent investigators."

Leo grinned weakly, his face flushing with color. As usual, he found compliments incredibly difficult to accept. Neither Leo nor Niki spoke for a few seconds. Outside, a car rumbled past.

Niki settled into an armchair facing Leo and bent forward, she rested her elbows on her knees. She fixed Leo with an intense, unwavering stare. "You know, you could just tell her," Niki said softly.

Leo narrowed his eyes a touch and tried to return Niki's penetrating stare. Their eyes locked, and he felt instantly uncomfortable. He looked away.

"Look, I know it's none of my business," Niki said, splaying her hands on the coffee table. "But I'm a few years older than you, and let's just say I have a little more experience in matters like this."

"I don't..." Leo said, but Niki raised a finger to silence him.

"Honestly, what you do about it is up to you. This is your life, obviously, but let's just talk honestly for a moment." Niki glanced at the door. "Before Allissa gets back."

Leo flushed, feeling vulnerable and conflicted. Succumbing to the power of Niki's intense stare, he nodded once.

"She's an amazing woman, right?" Niki asked, and her lopsided smile invited Leo's honestly.

"Yeah, of course. She's amazing."

"You think there's more to this than…"

"I don't know," Leo interrupted before Niki could label it anything. "We've never really talked about it."

"Listen," Niki said. "I've spent the last fifteen years working with relationships that have broken down. I've seen cheating partners, hidden lovers. Heck, I've even seen a whole hidden family once or twice."

Leo smiled.

"What I mean is, I think I know when there's something between two people."

"Yeah," Leo mumbled. He tried to turn away, but the pain in his shoulder wouldn't allow it. Leo chewed over unsaid words. He wanted to say how much Allissa brought to his life, that he loved the time they spent together, and how much he longed to be honest about it all. But, as usual, Leo remained silent.

"It's obvious to me that there is something between the pair of you," Niki said. "Whatever that is, I won't embarrass you by speculating. But I know this for certain: life's way too short to not act on things that mean so much."

Footsteps thumped up the stairs. Leo glanced anxiously at the door.

"I realize it's a lot to take in, and the time never seems right," Niki added hurriedly. "But you can spend your whole life waiting for the right time." Niki gazed off to one side as though she were looking at something in the past.

Allissa burst in through the door, a bag of takeout food swinging from one hand. She stopped and glanced from Leo to Niki and back again.

"What are you two talking about so intently?" Allissa asked, walking toward the table. She swept a few documents aside and dropped the food.

"We're talking about you, actually," Niki said, her tone as innocent as a newborn lamb.

Leo shot her a panicked look.

"We were talking about how long it would take you to come back with the food. I think you could have gone to China and fetched it in that time." Niki flashed Leo, who was now glowing a beetroot red, a glance.

Allissa smirked. "I didn't see you offering to help, being the native New Yorker and all."

"Hey, I was giving you a cultural experience. Sometimes you gotta get out from beneath the wings of 'old mother hen'." Niki glanced animatedly at her underarm.

"Problem is," Allissa said, pulling boxes out of the bag and laying them on the table. "There's just too much choice. So, I kept it simple and went for noodles."

As the danger of exposure passed, Leo's stomach rumbled. He stood slowly, padded toward the table, and assessed what Allissa had bought. Instantly hypnotized by the smell, he tore open the nearest box, grabbed a fork and dove straight in.

Niki selected hers and Allissa, the last. The three sat in silence for several minutes, munching away.

"What do we know about this killer?" Allissa said, collecting the three empty boxes. Niki rearranged the articles on the table and stood looking down at them. Colorful pictures of the young, beautiful, and unfortunate victims of the Downtown Ripper smiled up at her.

"He's opportunistic," Niki said. She laid out another printed article, then folded her arms.

Allissa examined the four victims. Three had lost their lives, and one — thanks to Leo — had survived.

"He?" Allissa questioned.

"It was definitely a man," Leo said. "You heard the description I gave to the police."

"I agree, it's most likely to be a man," Allissa said, pointing down at the images. "But can we be totally certain? We want to avoid unintentionally discounting anyone who might be the killer."

"I know what I saw," Leo said. He stood and walked across to the coffee machine.

"You need to rest," Alissa said, moving to intercept Leo. "I can do that for you."

"I might need to rest, but I can definitely manage to make a cup of coffee," Leo snapped, more aggressively than he intended. He twisted one of the dials and a torrent of steam hissed aggressively from the machine.

"Also, because the killings are so violent," Niki said, pointing down at a picture of one of the victims. "There's something about them that's sort of, animalistic."

"I don't know why we're even discussing this. I know what I saw," Leo said, poking a button. The machine hissed again, this time sending steam toward Leo's arm. He darted out of the way a second too late, earning a scald and a stab of pain from his shoulder.

"Women can be violent too," Niki said.

"This machine can be violent," Leo muttered, shaking his hand where the steam had caught him. "Okay, I give up. Niki, please come and help me with this before I throw it out of the window."

Niki and Allissa shared a glance, and both rolled their eyes.

"I might have an injured shoulder, but there's nothing wrong with my eyes!" Leo snapped, trying, but failing, to sound angry.

Niki strode across the room and deftly set about working the machine.

"While we're on the subject of your eyes," Allissa said. "You haven't got night vision, have you?"

"Na, I chose the ability to read minds instead. What's your point?"

"It was dark, and you didn't actually see the killer." Allissa placed her hands on her hips and rounded on Leo.

"Don't you start doubting me too," Leo said, eyeing Allissa and watching what Niki was doing with the machine at the same time.

"I'm not doubting you. I know it wasn't Andy. I'm just trying to be clear about what we do and don't know," Allissa said.

"The killer was around six-foot-one," Leo said. "He was significantly slimmer than Andy and much more muscular."

"Which suggests he's a man," Niki said, coaxing the smell of freshly brewed coffee into the office.

Even the scent of coffee acted as something of a salve to Leo. He rubbed his eyes and yawned. With the attack, then the night at the hospital, he'd had no sleep at all. Niki filled three cups, passed one to Leo, and carried the other two across to the table.

"The key to this is with the surviving victim," Allissa said. "She spent the most time with the killer."

"She hasn't been able to tell the police anything yet," Niki said. "She'd spent several hours drinking cocktails and can't remember anything specific. She was out on the town with friends, but they left her there. Just assumed she'd gone already."

"Nice people," Allissa said.

"Yeah," Niki agreed. "The friends can't remember who she was talking to, either."

"How do you know all of this?" Allissa said.

"It was on the news this morning." Niki pointed a thumb at the television. "Nothing stays out of the news in this city. Let's see if anything's changed." Niki tapped the remote and the 24-hour news station filled the screen. A reporter interviewed a man about last night's attempted murder.

"It's him again," Allissa said, pointing at the screen.

"Yeah," Niki agreed, "he's always on. I've no idea how he knows so much."

"I met him in the bar last night," Allissa said, remembering the meeting for the first time. "It was a couple of hours before... you know, what."

"Really?" Niki spun around and looked hard at Allissa. "You should have said..."

"I forgot about it with everything that went on after..."

"Did he say anything about the case?"

"He said he was swamped with all the interviews. At the time, we weren't looking for the killer, we just wanted to find Andy."

"Strange how much can change in a few hours," Leo muttered.

"I don't understand, why he would know anything about Andy?" Niki asked, looking hard at Allissa.

Allissa pointed at the screen. "His name's Seth. He was in the same bar the evening before, too. His office is nearby. I wondered whether he'd seen Andy there."

Niki tapped a pen against her chin.

"Anyway, I swapped numbers with Seth." Allissa pointed at the television. "He promised to get in touch if he remembered anything about the night before or ended up bumping into Andy." Allissa dug her phone out and glanced at it. "It was a long shot but..." she stopped talking and looked hard at Niki and then Leo. "Seth sent me a message this morning. He wants to meet later."

Niki looked at Allissa. "What did you say?"

"Nothing yet..."

Niki looked hard at Allissa, the cogs of her mind clearly working overtime.

"Whatever you're thinking, it's a really bad idea," Leo said, pointing at Niki. With the caffeine working its way through his system, he felt as though he were back in the real world again.

Niki and Allissa shared a long glance, and then both looked at Leo. No one spoke for several seconds, then Allissa stepped toward Leo.

"Seth clearly knows more than we do. I think it would be a good idea to meet him and see if I can get any insights."

"No way, it's not a good idea," Leo said, finishing the coffee. "We don't know who this guy is. We don't know that he's not involved. It might be dangerous." He was about to say the idea made him feel a rage of jealousy, but his voice ran dry.

"And what?" Niki cut in, with a knowing smile.

"It might be dangerous!" Leo repeated. He stretched his arms out, and the movement sent a jolt of pain through his body.

"It can't be any more dangerous than wrestling a serial killer to the ground," Niki said, her gaze locked on Leo. Leo returned the gaze and got the impression that the detective saw straight through his excuses.

"Oh, come on. Look at him," Allissa said, pointing at the man on the screen. "I met him last night. He was a nice guy. He bought me a beer and everything."

"Dangerous people don't go around advertising the fact,"

Leo said. "They don't wear shirts with *I'm Dangerous* printed on the front."

"I mean, if cheesy grins could kill," Niki said, shrugging. "But maybe Leo's right. Perhaps in the circumstances, it's not a good idea for you to go out alone." She locked eyes with Allissa.

Leo let out half a sigh of relief before Niki started speaking again.

"We will set it up so that you meet him in public. I'll always stay close by; you won't even see me. I'm good at blending in."

An image of Allissa beaming at Seth crashed headlong into Leo's mind. The jealous thoughts revved and roared, careening through the corners of his consciousness at breakneck speed.

"They won't be out of my sight even for a second," Niki said. "Allissa's just going to use that womanly charm of hers to see if this guy knows anything we don't."

"Doesn't... doesn't that make you question how he knows so much?" Leo stuttered.

"That's his job. He probably has informants in the police or something," Allissa replied.

"These reporters use all sorts of means to get information. He's a well-connected guy," Niki added.

"I understand that, but I just..." Leo's voice trailed off as he realized he had no legitimate reasons for Allissa not to spend a couple of hours with a man who was related to the case. Being jealous of her for spending time with a man who might or might not find her attractive was not a valid excuse.

"If we can get a step ahead," Niki said, her voice softening. "If we can just get something that puts us ahead, then we could solve this."

"Do you know how great that would be for us all?"

Allissa chimed in, playing her part in the persuasive tag team. "Imagine the publicity we'll get if we can tell people we beat the NYPD catching the Downtown Ripper."

Leo glanced from Niki to Allissa and back again. He tried to fold his arms tightly, but the wound hurt too much. "I'm not happy about it," he said.

"Clearly," Niki said, folding her arms more successfully than Leo had. Her voice was harder now. "Why might that be?"

Leo saw Niki's lopsided grin and blushed. He shrugged, not knowing how to answer the question.

"Honestly," Allissa said, "it'll be fine. I'm just going to talk to him and see if he knows anything. Niki will be close, so you don't need to worry."

"Okay, fine," Leo said. "But only if you stay in sight the whole time. We'll be less than two minutes away."

"Wait a second." Allissa pointed at Leo's shoulder. "You're under doctor's orders not to do anything..."

"Yeah, but," Leo tried to protest, but the movement sent another shockwave of pain through him.

The women shared a glance.

"You stay right here," Allissa said. "Niki will be nearby, and nothing will go wrong. Don't worry at all."

Allissa picked up her phone and typed a message. A reply came almost immediately.

"We're meeting at the Broadway-Lafayette Metro in thirty minutes."

22

ALLISSA HAD ALWAYS CONSIDERED herself a confident person. She'd traveled the world on her own, met dozens, maybe even hundreds of people, and faced all sorts of dangers without ever really being scared.

But now, waiting outside the Broadway-Lafayette Metro station, she felt a flurry of something akin to worry. Frowning, she thought about how reluctant Leo had been for her to meet Seth. Although Leo had conceded eventually, Allissa respected his instincts — in the past, those instincts had saved both their lives.

Allissa forced the worry away and pulled a smile in case Seth was nearby. She scanned people on the opposite side of the road, moving through the glow of a bright electronic billboard on the side of the building.

Niki was watching from somewhere over there, too, just to make sure nothing could go wrong.

Allissa shook her head and forced the thoughts away. Seth was a TV and social media star, not a killer. The guy might be overconfident and arrogant, but not dangerous.

Allissa spotted Seth climbing the stairs of the metro

station, reinforced her smile and banished the worries from her mind.

Seth noticed Allissa standing in the crowd and raised a hand. He cut a beeline through the milling people and greeted her with a kiss on each cheek.

"It's great to see you again," Seth said, flashing his unnaturally white smile.

"My pleasure," Allissa replied, trying to sound genuine. She didn't feel as though she achieved it, but she also doubted Seth noticed.

"Do you mind if we grab lunch?" Seth asked, touching his stomach. "I've been flat out all morning and haven't had a chance to eat."

"No problem. I could do with eating too," Allissa lied. In fact, she hated the idea of going to a restaurant, as that meant she would be socially obliged to stay with Seth the entire time. A coffee, on the other hand, could just be an hour at the max.

"Thanks, I know a great place nearby. This way." Seth led them away from the metro station. "It's been a busy few weeks."

"Sounds like it," Allissa said, remembering how much they needed information from this man. "Is your work always like this?"

"It comes and goes," Seth said. "I try to keep a work life balance, but I'm not sure I'm managing it this week."

"Tell me about your business, then?" Allissa acted dumb to warm Seth up with some simple questions.

"That way," Seth said, pointing them across the street. They turned left onto Bleecker Street. As they walked, Seth ran Allissa through the various things he did, making each one sound difficult and dangerous.

"Didn't you think about working for traditional news outlets?" Allissa said.

Seth laughed out loud. "I get asked that a lot." He giggled again, although Allissa couldn't see the funny side. "I have no problem with traditional news, TV, radio, and newspapers. They're great. They've got prestige, and quite frankly, I wouldn't be able to do what I do today if they hadn't set the foundations. But their time has passed."

"Why do you think that?" Allissa said. "Don't most people still get their information from the mainstream news services?"

"They just don't have the speed or the responsiveness that I do," Seth said. "Let me give you an example." They waited for a taxi to crawl past before crossing the road. When they were on the opposite pavement, Seth continued. "Traditional news people have to produce a set amount of content. If they have half an hour, they need to fill half an hour. If they have a hundred pages, they need to fill a hundred pages. I'm not like that."

"No?" Allissa asked, glancing up at him. His unblemished skin and high cheekbones gleamed somewhat unnaturally.

"No, I only write things that interest my readers. I don't just fill pages for the sake of it. All killer, no filler." Seth smiled at his joke.

Allissa thought of the sensationalized *Ten Worst Serial Killers of All Time* article she'd read an hour before but kept quiet.

"That makes sense, I suppose," she said. "What have you been working on this week?"

"Oh, it's been all about this *Downtown Ripper*. Have you heard of him?"

"I've seen a couple of headlines," Allissa said, turning to glance at Seth. "There's not been another victim, has there?"

"Yes, didn't you know? Last night. Well, an attempted one. Some hero fought him off."

"Wow," Allissa replied.

"Let's go here," Seth said, pointing at an Italian restaurant on the left. "One of my favorite places."

Seth shoved open the door and held it for Allissa to walk through. The restaurant was exactly the sort of place Allissa avoided. She glanced around at tables with linen covers, topped with glittering cutlery and a candle. The sound of piped piano music, and the gentle chatter of diners made her want to spin on her heel and get straight out of there. Allissa frowned, longing to be in somewhere more down to earth with Leo.

A server appeared and tried to direct Seth and Allissa to a table toward the back of the restaurant.

"Do you mind if we sit there?" Allissa said, pointing at a table in the window. "I'm not in the city for long, and just like to see the world go past."

If Seth cared, he didn't show it. The server led Allissa and Seth to the table and then delivered menus. Allissa glanced out through the glass and noticed that it had started to rain. She peered into the window of a café opposite and saw Niki settling into a table.

Seth continued talking about his website, despite Allissa not asking. In fact, Seth spoke about his website throughout the ordering process and was still on the topic when the food arrived. The server slid Allissa's salad onto the table. Having eaten an entire box of noodles recently, she wasn't hungry, but also didn't want to sit there with nothing.

"You know why I like this restaurant?" Seth said, picking up his knife and cutting into his sirloin steak. "They know how to do a rare steak. So often you ask for rare, and it comes medium. I mean, it's not that difficult. A couple of minutes on either side. But this," — he pointed at the meat from which blood oozed — "is perfect. Just perfect." He put it in his mouth and chewed.

Allissa picked up her fork and dug into the salad.

"What makes a great story for you?" Allissa asked, navigating the conversation away from Seth's multiple successes and toward the reason she was there — to find out about the Downtown Ripper. "What do your readers really go for?"

"They like the gritty stuff. They want to hear about the killer who did all kinds of bad stuff and got away with it." Seth cut and ate another mouthful of steak. "I'm not sure why, but people love to hear about those killers who've outsmarted the police."

"Everyone loves the underdog," Allissa said, chewing some leaves which didn't really taste of anything.

"That's true. I think that's probably why my stuff sells."

"Do you think this Downtown Ripper will be like that?" Allissa asked.

Seth's eyebrows rose as he chewed. He coughed, then took a sip of water.

"Well, I don't know for sure," he said. "But I can tell you this, he's certainly captured the public interest." Seth stuffed another chunk of meat into his mouth.

"He?" Allissa said nonchalantly.

Seth's eyes locked on Allissa's like a pair of heat-seeking missiles. He stopped chewing and swallowed a piece of steak. "Well, it's bound to be a man, obviously. Female serial killers are rare, and this bears all the classic hallmarks of masculine aggression. The pattern, the method, it's textbook."

"Such as?" Allissa prompted, sensing the irritation in Seth's voice.

Seth's eyes narrowed as he considered his next words. "Consider his selection of victims. Women, exclusively. Each within a particular age bracket..." His voice trailed off, leaving the implication hanging in the air like a chilling fog.

"You think his motivations are sexual?" Allissa chewed another leaf.

Seth stopped eating. The steak lay abandoned. A trickle of blood pooled across his plate.

Seth's fingers hesitated before picking up a blood-stained chip from the plate. "No. Well, I'm not certain," he murmured, his gaze distant as he weighed his thoughts. "But from what we've seen," he continued, placing the chip back down with deliberate care, "this killer's psychological profile is unique. There hasn't been another with such... singular focus. For him, it's not about the act itself. This isn't about the cold, methodical elimination of life." A dark tension flashed across Seth's face, which chilled Allissa to the core. "This is a power play, a way to assert dominance. The killing is merely the conclusion of a twisted psychological need. In a way, it's something that he feels compelled to do. It's like the way an artist must create art."

"That's so interesting. I can see why people pay you to talk about this stuff," Allissa said, purposefully sounding awestruck.

Seth sat up a little straighter at the compliment.

"In your expert opinion then," Allissa said, pointing her fork at Seth. "Because you've got to be one of the most knowledgeable people in the field. What sort of person are we looking for?"

Seth's brow darkened as he thought about his answer.

"Well, let's see. What do we know? He's quite a confident person."

"Why do you think that?"

"There doesn't appear to be any preexisting connection between him and the victims; at least, none that the authorities have uncovered so far." Seth's voice took on a reflective note. "That suggests he's encountering his victims spontaneously, selecting his targets only moments before he acts. It's opportunistic, impulsive—not the behavior of someone who plans extensively, but rather someone who thrives on the thrill of the immediate hunt."

Allissa nodded. "You think he just passes them on the street?"

Seth picked up his knife and fork again and sliced a chunk from the meat. "Yes, something like that, I imagine." He gesticulated with his steak knife. The serrated blade was stained with blood.

"He must be quite a young guy then," Allissa suggested.

"What makes you think that?"

"There's no sign that he's forced the women to go anywhere with him. None of them had any known history of prostitution. That makes me think he's persuading them to go with him voluntarily. I think it's more likely that he persuades a woman of a similar age to go with him, rather than someone younger."

"You're good at this," Seth said, nodding. "What do you say I get the check here and we head on somewhere a little more relaxing?"

Allissa glanced from Seth down to the bleeding hunk of meat on his plate.

"I have quite a lot of work on this..." Allissa said, starting with an excuse but then changing her mind. After all, the conversation with Seth had just become interesting. "Alright, just for another hour. Then I really do need to go back."

23

———

Leo sighed. His brain ached from the realizations of the day, and he felt sick at the thought of Allissa out there with another man. Then he thought of his sister and nephew, missing Andy while he was in jail.

Thinking of Andy, Leo strode over to the table on which the clear plastic bag containing Andy's personal possessions sat. Andy had been adamant that Leo took the possessions, mostly because he wanted to make sure the watch got back to Michael as quickly as possible. Leo wondered whether the act was a sign of change for Andy — for once, he seemed to worry about someone other than himself.

Leo slid his hand into the bag and pulled out the watch. Although Leo knew nothing about watches, he had to admit that this looked like a nice one. He turned it side to side and the polished platinum casing caught the light with an understated opulence. He would make sure to hand the watch back to Michael as soon as possible.

Leo placed the watch down and turned his attention to the other items in the bag. He drew out a fold of crumpled bills and leafed through them — just under two-hundred dollars. Of the two thousand dollars Andy had taken from his brother's apartment, he had either lost or spent over eighteen hundred dollars.

After digging out the few coins, and a packet of gum, Leo had expected the bag to be empty. Looking closely, he noticed a thin metal chain lying right at the bottom of the clear plastic bag. He drew the bag close to his face and turned it side to side. The chain glimmered. The chain had almost been hidden in the plastic fold at the bottom of the bag. Leo drew it out carefully and examined it in the light. The length indicated that it was designed to be worn around the wrist, although the clasp looked like it had split.

Frowning, he examined the piece. In all the years he'd known Andy, he hadn't remembered him ever wearing a chain like this one. Leo thought about Andy for a moment and considered the sort of jewelry Andy might wear. A chunky chain around his neck, maybe, but not this dainty gold bracelet.

Leo ran the chain through his fingers and noticed that mud caked several of the links. Leo wiped the chain carefully against his sleeve and wondered why the thing had become so filthy.

Leo grabbed his phone, took a picture of the chain, and sent it to Emma. She would know whether Andy owned something like this. The reply came quickly.

Nope. Andy doesn't wear anything on his wrist.

Leo frowned, then placed the chain down on the table. He exhaled and placed a hand across his injured shoulder. Tiredness and the hazy effect of the painkillers squirmed behind his eyes. Leo couldn't seem to hold a simple train of thought, let alone figure out something like this.

Andy had been out of his mind drunk for two days, Leo

remembered. Andy could have bought, found, or stolen the chain easily in that time.

Leo stretched his aching muscles and then instantly regretted it as a sharp pain seared through his shoulder. He winced, then checked the time and decided it was time for some more painkillers. He pulled the packet from his pocket and took two straight away. Then, in an attempt to still his spinning mind, Leo slumped into the sofa and thumbed the television remote. He hoped that the friendly chatter would help drown out his thoughts. The TV glowed, and the 24-hour news station appeared on the screen. Using his non-dominant hand to keep the pain away, Leo fumbled with the remote until the volume increased.

The Downtown Ripper attempted to claim his fourth victim last night. The voice of a news anchor-man filled the room.

Leo groaned and tried to change the channel. He stabbed at the control, but nothing happened.

Whoever the ripper is, the anchorman continued, *he's quickly becoming one of New York's most prolific serial killers. Two days ago, crime expert Seth Stryker said this...*

The image of the news presenter faded, and Seth appeared on the screen.

"This guy has no shame," Leo groaned when it became clear Seth was talking in front of one of the crime scenes. Yellow tape strung between the buildings fluttered in the breeze.

"Or respect," Leo added, watching Seth lap up the publicity of the news cameras as a woman lay dead.

"This is the last thing I need to see." Leo changed the angle of the remote to help it communicate with the screen. His finger slid over the required button, then he froze. He saw something on the screen that caused his hand to tremble. His arm dropped to the sofa beside him, and he shuffled forward. He tried to breathe, but suddenly it felt as though the air had been sucked from the room.

This is the scene in which... Seth droned on, but Leo wasn't listening. It wasn't the content of the conversation that shocked him, though. It wasn't even the senseless self-promotion of the man himself.

Leo bolted out of the sofa, and rushed across to the table, sending several bits of paper flying to the floor in his draft. White hot pain seared through his body with the movement, but he didn't even notice it. He grabbed the bracelet, then rushed back to the sofa and grasped the remote. It took him several attempts to pause the program.

Leo padded up to the screen, holding the bracelet aloft. His eyes swiveled from the chain to the screen and back again, growing bigger each time.

In the interview, Seth's sleeves were rolled up. Leo could see, glimmering in the New York winter sun of two days ago, as clear as day, what looked like the same chain he now held in his hands.

FROM HER VANTAGE point in the café across the street, Niki fixed her gaze on the front window of the Italian restaurant. Through the rain streaked the glass, she had a clear view of Allissa and Seth.

Niki had watched Allissa and Seth go inside and then breathed a sigh of relief when they appeared at the table in the window. Allissa glanced out into the street, giving Niki no doubt she had chosen the table on purpose.

Niki sipped her mint tea and thought about the conversation she had with Leo an hour before. As often happened when she was alone, Niki's mind slipped back into the past. The soft clink of coffee cups and the murmur of subdued café conversations echoed around her, relaxing her into the thoughts.

Movement across the street dragged Niki out of her reverie. She rocked forward, her eyes instantly snapping into focus.

Seth climbed to his feet and disappeared into the restaurant. Thirty seconds later, Allissa rose to her feet and followed. Whatever was going on in there, Niki didn't like it. She left a few bills on the table and swiftly made her exit.

Niki charged out into the rain and sprinted across the road. A car hit the brakes and screeched to a stop a foot away. Niki didn't even notice, crashing headlong through the restaurant's front door. Diners glanced at her as she entered, as though she were a different species entirely. Niki turned one way, then the other, looking frantically for Allissa and Seth. She couldn't see them.

The place was quiet. A piano tinkled somewhere, and the sound of dinnertime conversation bubbled.

Niki marched over to the nearest server. "I need to know where the people who were eating at that table went," Niki demanded, pointing at the table in the window where Allissa and Seth had been two minutes before.

"Sorry, I'm just serving these gentlemen —"

Niki wedged herself between the server and his diners, then pulled the notepad from his hands. "You can do that later. I need to know about those people right now," Niki said. "It's urgent!"

A hush settled over the restaurant as diners flashed Niki an awkward glance.

"They left about two minutes ago," said a man from the table next to where Allissa and Seth had been. "I saw them. They used the other door. It exits on the other street." The man pointed further into the restaurant."

Niki cursed herself for forgetting that this restaurant occupied a corner and had exits on both sides.

"Thanks," Niki hissed. She forced the server's notepad back into his hands and rushed through the restaurant. Inside, the restaurant was deceptively big. Servers moved sedately between candle-lit tables. She charged around a server carrying steaming plates of food and almost upset one of the linen-clad tables.

Niki reached the rear door and grabbed a server by the shoulder. "Two people left this way?"

"Sure," the server said, offering a brief description. "Just a couple of minutes ago. They wanted a taxi. You might just catch them."

Niki burst out into the New York downpour; her figure was immediately enveloped by the relentless rain. She watched as the lights of a taxi painted long, luminescent streaks of red across the wet asphalt. The cab signaled and turned right at the far end of the street, its taillights fading into the dense curtain of rain.

Niki clenched her hands into tight fists. She spun around, her heart pounding a frantic rhythm inside her ribs. She pulled out her phone and called Allissa. The phone rang several times, but nothing happened. Standing still for a moment, Niki heard the rumble of a nearby phone vibrating. A feeling of dread worked its way through her throat.

She did a three-sixty, trying to work out where the sound was coming from. Following the vibrating sound, Niki stepped toward an olive bush beside the door. She peered behind the pot. The feeling of dread became an all-out physical sickness. Allissa's phone sat behind the pot, vibrating frantically.

Niki picked up Allissa's phone and ended the call. Then, she dialed Leo.

THE REALIZATION SMASHED Leo like a sledgehammer to his guts. He gripped on to the table for support as the room spun around him. If he was thinking clearly, he would have put it down to the strong painkillers, but his thoughts were already way past that. For almost ten seconds he stood, rooted to the spot, his gaze panning from the image on the screen to the bracelet that dangled between his fingers.

Leo spun around and eyed the door like a sprinter on the blocks. He was about to take flight, but he froze again.

"Could there be another, more reasonable explanation?" Leo whispered. In his mind's eye, he imagined Allissa saying it.

He thought about how embarrassed he would be if he charged into the situation without working it out properly. He forced himself to take five long and slow breaths, somewhat calming his pounding heart rate, and forcing logical thought back into his consciousness.

"What do I know for certain?" Leo said, rubbing a hand across his face. "I need to be certain." He glanced around, momentarily self-conscious that someone might know he was talking to himself. "If Colombo can talk to himself, then Leo Keane's got no problems," he added.

Leo ran the bracelet through his fingers again and studied it with much greater attention than before. Then he walked right up to the screen, his face just inches from the pixels, and studied it. Whilst the image was small and a little blurry, the bracelets certainly looked the same.

Leo straightened up and gazed at the screen. *Seth Stryker — True Crime Blogger,* the overlaid banner said.

"That's not enough," Leo muttered. "I need more." Running the bracelet through his fingers, he noticed that there was a tiny gold plate in the center of the chain. The plate was barely larger than the chain itself, and as such, almost indistinguishable, if you didn't look closely.

Leo examined the plate. It looked as though something was written on it, although he couldn't make it out. He paced across to the window, where daylight streamed through. Although he could see the engraving more clearly here, he still couldn't make out what he said. It looked as though the words had been weathered away from years of use.

Leo placed the bracelet on the windowsill and took out his phone. He got as close as he could while the camera was still in focus and took a photo of the engraving. He used the phone's edit mode to zoom in on the photo. He then increased the contrast to give him a better view of the engraved name. As Leo read the name, a wave of realization crashed over him, swiftly followed by a torrent of new questions.

William Stryker.

He launched a web browser and typed in the name. Profiles for various William Strykers emerged, dotting the globe. One profile belonged to a businessman in Massachusetts, another to a minister from an obscure place Leo had never heard of. This seemed increasingly like a wild goose chase. Leo scrolled down again and saw another entry. This one captured Leo's attention. He tapped the screen and waited for the page to load painstakingly slowly. When it finally did, Leo read the text aloud.

"William Stryker 1832-1896, a New York-based doctor and entrepreneur who became infamous after being accused of the Jack the Ripper killings in London in 1889."

Leo gasped and looked up from the screen. His eyes set on Seth's image, frozen mid-explanation. After two seconds he returned to the article.

"Stryker built a large medical business and was in London in the fall when the killings occurred. Before they could arrest him, he fled back to New York. Scotland Yard could not find enough evidence to extradite Stryker to

London, but with the publicity surrounding the allegations, Stryker's business collapsed. He died in poverty five years later."

Leo inhaled. "William Stryker could be Seth's great-great-grandfather or something like that." Leo's mind was running in overdrive now. "No wonder he has such an interest in historical crimes. But what are the similarities between the killings?"

He ran across to the table on which Allissa and Niki had laid out information about the murders so far. "Four victims so far, all women." Fingers slipping easily over his phone, Leo looked up the names of Jack the Ripper's victims.

"Five known Ripper victims," he read out loud. "Mary Ann Nichols, Anne Chapman... no, that can't be right." He checked the names of Seth's victims, but none matched up.

"Wait, wait," Leo said, momentarily forgetting about his injury and poking at the table. "Where were the bodies found?"

His fingers flew over the screen again. The search results loaded at an agonizingly slow speed. "They discovered Mary Ann Nichols on Friday 31st of August in Buck's Row. A week later, Annie Chapman on Hanbury Street. Elizabeth Stride in Dutfield's yard." Leo prodded at the screen, unable to verbalize his realization.

"Seth killed his first victim beside Dr Buck's cosmetic surgery," Leo said. "The second outside Hanbury's clothes shop, the third beside Dutfield's Diner."

He read in silence for a few more seconds.

"Then there was Miter Square," he said. "I stopped the murder in Washington Square. But where now?"

Leo's train of thought derailed abruptly as his phone erupted into a shrill ring, startling him so intensely that the device nearly slipped from his grasp. Recovering quickly, he swiped the screen and pressed the phone to his ear, instantly recognizing Niki's voice. The undercurrent of distress in her tone was unmistakable. A ring of muscle tightened around Leo's heart.

"They've gone!" was all Niki said.

25

———————

"WHAT DO YOU MEAN, they've gone?" Leo asked, down the line. "You were supposed to be watching them the whole time."

"I was watching the restaurant from across the street," Niki shouted above the pounding rain. "Seth got up. I assumed he was going to the restrooms, so thought nothing of it. Then Allissa got up, and no one came back. The restaurant had another door. They went out that way."

Leo's vision clouded and his heart slammed against his ribs. He needed to think. His chest tightened. His breathing became frantic. Anxiety threatened to suffocate him. He leaned against the wall and fought for control.

"Allissa is a strong person; she's not going to..." Niki said.

"You don't understand," Leo shouted down the phone. "It's Seth! Seth is the ripper. He's the one killing these women."

Niki listened in stunned silence, and Leo explained his realizations. When he'd finished, Niki continued to say nothing.

"Are you still there?" Leo said. "You're not going to try to tell me I'm wrong or overreacting."

When Niki spoke, her voice was as cold as arctic ice. "We need to work out where he's taken her."

Leo closed his eyes tight. He knew Allissa was a feisty, fiery young woman who, alongside Leo, had faced down the barrel of a gun. A feeling in his gut told him that this was different. Leo knew, almost beyond a doubt, that Seth was a serial killer, and was now in a taxi going somewhere with Allissa. A serial killer who intended for her to be his next victim.

"Leo, listen to me." Niki's voice pulled Leo back into action. "You say this is all linked to the places where the murders took place?"

"Yes, that's what it looks like."

"Where did Jack the Ripper murder the next victim?

Leo clicked on the speakerphone function and swiped back to his internet search. "13 Miller's Court," he said. "Mary Jane Kelly was murdered at Thirteen Miller's Court."

"Right." Niki's voice became distant for a few seconds. "You'll never guess what…"

"There's an apartment building called Miller's Court," Leo interrupted, having just completed the same search.

"It's two miles from me," Niki said. "I'll be there in less than five minutes at this time of night. Stay by the phone. I'll be in touch soon."

The line went dead.

NIKI TYPED Miller's Court into the taxi app. The system loaded, and then told her that the nearest car was six minutes away. The three minutes since Allissa and Seth's taxi had sloshed away already felt like hours.

"It shouldn't be long. There're always taxis around here," Niki said through clenched teeth. She paced across the sidewalk and looked one way and then the next.

The throaty drone of a motorbike echoed between the buildings somewhere. Tires swished across the wet road as a car passed out of sight.

The street was dark and motionless. In a city of thirteen thousand taxis, she was on the only street without one.

Niki glanced at the taxi arrival countdown as though it was a bomb detonation.

Niki hunched her shoulders and exhaled. She spun around again. Adrenaline rattled through her. She'd never had problems like this when she was tailing cheating partners through the backstreets. That long, boring, but lucrative work had never been this high pressure.

An engine growled, and a horn ricocheted through the sheets of rain.

The door of the restaurant whispered open, and a couple peered out. Sounds of the restaurant rattled incongruously into the street. A tinkling piano played a cheerful jazz tune, and diners chattered.

"Hey, Maurice, where's our taxi? We had it booked for five minutes ago," the woman at the door said.

"It'll be with you shortly ma'am," the server replied.

The orange halo of a taxi's lights slid around the corner. They shone from the dulled windows of a dozen shops.

"I need that taxi, sorry." Niki charged for the taxi; her arms raised above her head. She stomped through a puddle to block the taxi's progress.

The taxi squealed to a stop, and the driver pulled down his window. "I'm booked," he said.

"It's an emergency," Niki yelled. "I need to get to Miller's Court quickly."

"Not with me, miss. I'm booked." The driver edged the car forward.

Niki stood in front of the taxi to prevent it from moving.

"You know the rules, miss. I'm booked!" the driver yelled.

"Fifty dollars for a ten-minute journey," Niki said, pulling out a bill.

"Can't do it. Now get out of the way." The driver edged the car further forward.

"One hundred then," Niki shouted.

The driver paused and registered Niki's determined expression.

"Sure, okay," he relented, finally unlocking the doors.

"Quick as you can." Niki slid into the back seat.

The woman who'd booked the taxi scowled from the restaurant's door.

"What's the hurry?" the driver said as he examined Niki in the rear-view mirror.

"If I told you, you wouldn't believe me." Niki dug out another fifty. "I'll give you another fifty if you step on it."

"Yes, ma'am." The driver accepted the notes and punched the accelerator.

Niki stared from the taxi as the streets of New York flashed past.

She thought of Leo back at the office and realized that he must be going out of his mind with worry.

Then Niki thought of the unspoken words hanging between Leo and Allissa. She'd sensed it from the first time they'd met. Tension like that could mean only one thing.

Niki grabbed her phone and dialed the emergency number. "Yes, NYPD. What's your emergency?"

Niki wasn't sure the police would take it seriously. It all sounded so far-fetched, but she had to try.

The call connected, and Niki explained everything as concisely as she could.

A row of shuttered shops flashed past. People queued outside a nightclub. Warm lights glowed from apartment buildings and offices. All around the city, life was going on as usual. Yet in apartment thirteen at Miller's Court, something awful was about to happen.

"Come on, come on," Niki said, finally hanging up the phone. Not getting there in time was not an option.

26

"Two miles is too far. That'll take too long," Leo hissed, pacing across the office. The pain in his shoulder had returned to a white-hot slicing sensation every time he moved. So much for staying still, he thought.

He used his phone to check the location of Miller's Court. At first, the map showed the whole of Manhattan, before zooming in to Miller's Court. As the map grew larger, Leo saw a pulsing blue dot just a few blocks away from Miller's Court.

It took Leo just three seconds to calculate the distance. He was much closer to Miller's Court than Niki, and probably closer than the police. He tapped the screen and calculated the distance. At a slow run, Leo figured he could be there in less than ten minutes.

Leo glanced down at his shoulder and winced. Injury or not, Allissa's life was on the line, and doing nothing was not an option. Leo studied the map for ten seconds to memorize the location. Constantly checking the location would slow him down. When he was confident he knew the route, Leo slipped the phone in his pocket, tightened his shoes, and ran for the stairs.

Taking the stairs two at a time, Leo pushed out through the door and ran into the rain.

"I know I can run this," Leo groaned, biting down against the pain. He was used to running more than ten times this distance every day — although that was without the injury.

He reached the first corner, remembered the directions, and barreled to the left. A young couple leaped out of the way just in time to avoid a collision. His knees ached with the vibrations through the thin soles of his shoes that weren't designed for running. Each shudder sparked a fresh wave of pain from his shoulder. He pushed the pain away, closed his eyes to slits, and concentrated on forcing his way forward.

He surged harder with each throbbing step. The sweat came. His arms pumped. Images of Allissa and Seth bombarded his mind. A car pulled out of a side street ahead. Leo charged in front of it. There was no time to stop. The driver protested on the horn, but the sound drifted away in the city's restless noise.

Leo pushed harder still, and his legs finally normalized to the movement. His breathing dropped into sync. With every step, a searing agony lanced through his muscles, and the intense throb of his wounds saturated his consciousness.

Ten minutes had passed when Leo finally neared the last stretch to Miller's Court. The rain had drenched him to the bone, his clothes clinging to his skin and soaking his bandage so that it rubbed against the wound.

For the first time since stepping out into the rain, Leo checked the map and saw that Miller's Court was just ahead on the right. He raised his gaze to the towering monolithic structure that soared into the brooding New York sky. The building's austere façade, a tapestry of uniform gray, stood stark against the clouds. Here and there, windows pierced the darkness with warm, yellow light, but the shadow cloaked most of the building.

Leo ran across the road and into the gloomy street. Other than the distant rumble of traffic and the pounding rain, everything was quiet. He glanced at the map again and realized that a taxi might have taken a more circuitous route, with one-way systems and traffic signals.

Leo ran on, dodging a mound of trash, the swerve sending a lance of fresh agony radiating through his wounded shoulder. He reached the entrance and paused. The sight of the sign, *Miller's Court,* etched in letters that time had rendered almost illegible, sent a fresh surge of unease through him.

Leo stepped up to the door and glanced into the gloomy foyer. His breath billowed in great clouds and misted on the glass. A green emergency light washed the place in an eerie glow.

Rainwater trickled inside the collar of his coat, sending an involuntary shiver down his spine.

Leo pulled the handle, but the door didn't move. He turned to the door's entry system's twinkling buttons on the wall to the right. Some glowed faintly, and others were dull. The one in the top right corner flickered and then died. Some residents had taped their name beside a button. Leo searched for apartment 13 and found it blank.

The lights inside the foyer suddenly flickered to life, dazzling him. He squinted through the steamy glass. A grey-haired woman in a long coat shuffled toward the door. A small dog trotted beside her. She opened the door, muttering to herself, and stepped out into the night.

Leo slid his foot between the door and the jamb. The woman wandered away without looking back. She turned down the street and disappeared into the gloom. Leo slipped inside.

The hallway was cold and smelled damp. Yellowed paper fluttered from a notice board, and a sign on the far wall told Leo to turn left for flats 10-15.

Leo turned into the grey-walled corridor. His wet shoes squeaked across the floor.

A bulky radiator clanged, dripping water into a bucket that was almost overflowing.

Leo passed the door for flat 10 on the left and flat 11 on the right.

The building was quiet. A light further down the corridor blinked on and off a few times before deciding that off was easier.

Leo neared flat 13 and slowed. Each footstep felt grave and critical, as though he was playing on the knife's edge of success or failure. In his mind's eye, Leo pictured the first time he had met Allissa in Kathmandu. Then he recalled the stress of their cases in

Hong Kong and Berlin. Leo knew without a doubt that he wouldn't have survived any of the situations they had found themselves in without Allissa by his side.

Then he remembered all the evenings of laughter they'd shared on the sagging sofa in their dingy Brighton flat. Whether any of those things would happen again, Leo realized, was down to whatever now lay behind this door.

Leo stopped and studied the door. It was blue like the others in the hallway. The only thing to tell the doors apart were the discolored chrome numbers. The number three's highest screw had failed, causing the number to tilt backward.

Leo drew a deep breath and forced himself to focus. Before meeting Allissa, Leo's anxiety had run riot. Back then, he had struggled to talk to people on the phone, meet strangers, and sometimes even leave the house. That previous life seemed disconnected from him now, on the trail of a serial killer to save the woman he...

The entrance door slammed behind him, interrupting his thoughts. Leo's head whipped around. The woman with the dog walked back through the foyer and turned the opposite way.

Leo pictured Allissa once again. Then he saw the killer's blade. He fought for a deep breath. He needed to stay clear-headed and focused now. Everything depended on it. He couldn't let that happen to Allissa.

Leo leaned against the door and listened. A slam rang out through the building, but flat 13 was silent — as silent as a grave.

27

———

"Where is this place?" Allissa said, following Seth out of the taxi. On the way across the city, she had decided that she'd learned enough. She would have a drink with Seth so as not to raise suspicion, and then call it a night. "It must be a well-kept secret if it's on a street like this."

"Yes, it is." Seth led them further into the gloom. "It's one of those places very few people know about. A gem of a place. It's historical too."

Behind them, the taxi clunked into gear and swished off into the rain.

"Right," Allissa said. She squinted into the shadows but couldn't see anything that looked like a bar. A light above a shop flickered on and then died.

They walked further, passing a downpipe that sang as it channeled rainwater into the sewers.

"Just up here," Seth said, dropping behind Allissa on the narrow pavement.

Allissa saw something ghostly move in her peripheral vision. She spun to face the specter and saw a jet of steam rise through a grate in the middle of the street. Somewhere far away, the shriek of a siren echoed like a mating call through the concrete jungle.

Allissa squinted through the rain. A large concrete residential building reared upwards. Lights shone through the rain-streaked windows as residents hid from the rain behind filthy curtains. Beyond that, the road ended with a brick wall. Something scurried beneath a pile of rubbish.

Allissa stared up at the building. Its six-story concrete outline loomed tall against the sky. The name — *Miller's Court* — crowned the entrance in discolored letters. Lights from the door entry system winked.

The sirens were getting closer now. Allissa wondered where they were going.

"We must have gone the wrong way," Allissa said. She glanced to the side and noticed that Seth wasn't there. She spun around and realized that he'd dropped behind her, walking in single file even though the street was wide enough for them to stay side by side. As Allissa turned, her eyes focusing on Seth, she saw him whip his hand behind his back. The suspicious gesture made it look as though he were hiding something. His eyes glinted in some far-away light, looking like burning coals.

Allissa suddenly felt very alone. She shivered subconsciously and pulled her bag in close. Her hand instinctively moved toward her bag and the safety of her phone inside.

A crash from the building behind her startled Allissa. She whipped around, her muscles tensed. Scanning the shadows, she noticed a window on the second floor flapping in the wind. The wind abated for a moment and the sound of a late-night chat show streamed from the apartment. An inane television audience laughed at the same joke for the thousandth time.

Her senses now rattled. Allissa pictured herself and Leo

back in their hotel room, watching something mindless on the television.

"I think… I'm going to call it a night," Allissa said, eyeing Seth and then the main road behind. Without realizing she was doing it, she calculated how long it would take her to run to the safety of the main road. Thirty seconds maybe, Allissa decided. Her point was reinforced by a taxi swishing past like a physical link to safety and normality.

"Oh, I'm not sure you should do that," Seth said, his voice was calm and deep.

Allissa stared at him for a long moment, the voice not sounding as though it came from the same man. "I think you'll come with me." Seth grinned and his teeth sparkled menacingly.

"Like hell, I will," Allissa said, sliding her hand inside her bag. Her fingers explored the contents of the bag, looking for her phone. It was time to call Niki and get out of here as soon as possible. Allissa felt the shape of her purse, and a few other items, but no phone. Her search turned frantic as she sorted through the contents of the bag again. A surge of panic rose as she confirmed the one thing, she needed most wasn't there. She peered into her bag's depths with a growing sense of desperation.

"I think you'll find you left your phone back at the restaurant," Seth hissed. He stepped closer, his hand still hidden behind his back. His face twisted into a grin.

Another car swished down the road behind Seth. The headlight washed him in a milky glow for a second, before draining away.

Allissa narrowed her eyes. She shook her head slowly, covering her expression of fear with annoyance.

"You know what, you've got weirder by the second," Allissa said. "No wonder you like talking about dead people so much." Steeling her confidence and forcing herself into action, Allissa stepped around Seth and strode as quickly as she could without running toward the main road. Her heart pounded with a fear she refused to show.

"There's only so much time with weirdos I can take," she muttered.

She took two steps toward the main road, which was just one hundred feet away. Just as Allissa's foot poised to take a third step, a sudden, vice-like grip encircled her shoulder. With a swift, jarring tug, she was yanked backward. Her heart leaped within her chest and her muscles tensed, ready to fight back.

"What are you doing?" Allissa shouted. "Get your hands off me." She pushed against the arm, but Seth was surprisingly strong. His arm closed more tightly around her and pulled her backward.

Allissa dug her heels in, trying to pull away from Seth. Her feet slipped across the wet road. Seth yanked her even harder, pulling her backward and causing her to stumble.

"Let go, now!" Allissa shouted, swinging an elbow backward. She hit something that felt like a brick wall.

Not even acknowledging the blow, Seth tightened his grip and pulled Allissa against his chest. Allissa felt the steady beat of Seth's heart through her ribs.

"What are you doing?" she snarled. Her hands balled into fists. "Let go of me now."

Allissa swung her right fist over her shoulder. It hit nothing but air. She tried again with her left elbow. It struck something. She went for it again. The elbow crunched, and Seth grunted.

"Let go of me, now!" Allissa shouted as loud as she could, to attract the attention of someone nearby. "Let go of me or you'll regret it, you freak."

Seth's breath was heavy and warm on her neck.

Allissa changed tactics and stopped pulling away. She pushed back into Seth instead. He fell off balance and stumbled backward. He took two steps, dragging Allissa all the way. His grip around Allissa's neck stayed strong.

They struck a wall. Seth groaned. Allissa felt the impact through his ribcage. Not resting for a moment, Allissa went on the attack. She crashed her right elbow into his face and was about to go for a third when she stopped dead.

Something sharp, clean, and cold pressed against her neck. Allissa knew instinctively what it was — a knife. The pressure was light, but Seth held the blade firmly. Allissa stopped struggling and tried to force herself to relax. Any movement now, and she was likely to move the blade further into her neck.

"You know what's going to happen now," Seth said. "It's all you've wanted to talk about all night."

Allissa searched the street with wild eyes, looking for any movement. She longed to see a passing vehicle or person. The window above them closed and the noise of the TV muted.

"It's you," Allissa said. "You're..."

"Surprise," Seth whispered, nuzzling his lips against her cheek. He inhaled and grunted with pleasure. "I've been looking forward to this. We're going down in history together."

28

"MILLER'S COURT, just down there on the right." The taxi driver skidded to a stop and pointed down a side street. A large concrete building jutted up into the night.

Niki leaped out of the taxi and heard the somber shriek of sirens wailing through the city. Niki hoped they were coming this way and that the police had taken her seriously. In Niki's experience of dealing with the NYPD, they took things private investigators reported with a large pinch of salt.

"Allissa!" Niki shouted. "Are you here?"

Niki raced forward and looked around the street. The place was silent and deserted. Niki sloshed through the puddles, running into the looming shadow of Miller's Court. She glanced up at the structure; the rain falling almost vertically down at her and noticed that most of the building's windows were dull. A scarcely occupied place like this would be perfect for whatever atrocities Seth had planned, Niki realized.

She charged on toward the door and then froze. In the

gloom a few feet from the door, she saw something move. Standing still and forcing herself to breathe quietly, she heard feet shuffling across the pavement. Then she heard a muted voice, followed by a dull thump.

"Allissa!" Niki shouted again.

Niki rummaged through her bag, pulled out a flashlight, and snapped it on. The beam of light leaped across the space, illuminating the figures that had previously been obscured in the shadows. When Niki registered what she saw, her stomach fell to the floor. She gasped audibly and took a small step forward.

Stiff and ashen-faced, Allissa stood by the door. Her gaze met Niki's, conveying a silent scream of terror that words could not express.

Behind her loomed Seth, pressing the cold, sharp edge of a blade against the delicate skin of her neck. A sinister smile spread across his face, revealing a set of teeth that caught the stray light and gleamed menacingly. All the while, the distant wail of sirens grew increasingly louder, a haunting soundtrack to the unfolding nightmare.

"Seth, it's over," Niki said. "You can hear the police. They'll be here any moment."

"It's not over." Seth laughed. "I don't know if you've noticed, but I have a knife against her throat."

Allissa ducked backward and twisted, earning herself an inch of freedom. She ducked and then swung an elbow into Seth's ribs. The blow landed well, causing Seth to grunt.

Registering the opportunity, Niki shot forward, aiming to grab Seth's hand, which held the knife. Before Niki could close the gap, Seth reacted. He pulled Allissa back into position, looping his left hand around her neck. Then he drew the knife up to the side of her throat with his right.

Allissa stopped wriggling, and Niki froze. Now just six feet away, she could see the indentation of Allissa's skin beneath the blade.

"We know who you are, and we know about your great-grandfather," Niki said.

"Enough talking," Seth said, grinning wildly. "I know you're trying to waste my time. And before you state the obvious, I know I will not get away with it. I know you'll have this place surrounded within ten minutes, blah blah blah." Seth took a step backward, dragging Allissa toward the door to the building.

"Then give it up now," Niki said.

Seth laughed, although the sound was merely a strange gurgling sound from deep in his throat. "You don't understand. This was never about getting away with something, this was around *creating* something." Seth's eyes glimmered more menacingly now.

Allissa tried to speak, but the knife against her throat thwarted any sound.

Seth closed in on the door, dragging them through a puddle.

The shrill cry of police sirens sounded off the surrounding high-rise buildings, heralding the imminent arrival of the police.

"You don't have to do this," Niki said, glancing around. Her voice took on a softer tone. "I can help you get away. The police haven't worked it out yet. You let her go, and I'll get us all out of here."

"Haven't you been listening?" Seth snarled. "I don't want to get away with this. I want people to know this is me. This is my legacy, my family's legacy. I have it set up and ready. An article is scheduled to be published on my website in which I admit it all. I will not only be one of the most successful serial killers of all time, but I will also be one of the most famous people in the world!" Seth's eyes moved wildly from Niki to Allissa and back again.

The sirens whined again, drawing ever closer.

"I'm sorry I don't have time to chat," Seth said, edging toward the door. "I've got far too much riding on this to let you ruin it." Seth yanked Allissa backward again until they were beside the door. In one swift move, Seth withdrew his arm from around Allissa's neck and tapped an electronic key against the lock. The lock disengaged.

Allissa tried to say something. The knife against her throat stymied her words. Seth dragged her backward again.

"Save your energy." Seth looped his arm around Allissa's neck and pulled up against the door.

"Leo," Allissa muttered.

"He's not here, I'm afraid," Seth said. "It's only me now. We're doing this my way."

Seth shoved the door open and dragged Allissa inside. Lights in the entrance hall clicked on, showing the decrepit space in all its faded glory. Seth walked through a pile of abandoned junk mail, skittering the envelopes across the floor.

"Don't even think about moving," Seth said, wiggling the knife. The blade dug into Allissa's neck and a tiny rivulet of blood ran across her skin.

Seth stepped backward again and let the door swing closed. The lock engaged, trapping Niki outside.

Seth backed further into the foyer, dragging Allissa deeper into the building. He reached the back of the foyer, turned left, and disappeared out of Niki's sight.

Niki, dizzy with fear, rushed forward, and yanked at the

door. She pulled the handle, but the door didn't even move. She tried again, but the door was clearly impenetrable to anyone without a key. She banged on the glass with her fist.

"Someone, open this door!" she shouted, her breath misting on the glass, but got no reply.

29

———

THE DOOR to the foyer banged open, and footsteps jostled inside. Leo glanced toward the noise. He heard raised voices echo down the bare corridor. Leo recognized Niki's voice and instinctively ducked, as though ready for a fight.

The door swung closed, and Niki's voice sunk. A dull thump reverberated down the hallway as Niki pounded on the door. The door rattled against the jamb, the lock clearly sealing Niki on the outside.

Footsteps thumped and shuffled across the floor, getting louder. Leo realized he was the first one here, but Seth and Allissa were coming his way. His body tensed and his heart thundered. Pain still radiated from his shoulder, although Leo pushed it away. His eyes roamed the corridor for something he could use as a weapon. Apart from the doors to the other apartments, the corridor offered him nothing.

Then, looming like a specter from a nightmare, Seth's dark silhouette filled the hallway. Against the bright lights, Seth's frame cast a long shadow which reached across the floor toward Leo like a demonic a skeletal hand.

Leo stood rooted to the spot, watching Seth shuffle

closer. Then, pulling a deep breath, Leo forced himself into action.

Rising to the balls of his feet, Leo strode toward Seth. So far, Seth was facing Niki and moving backward toward the apartment. With his back to Leo, Seth clearly hadn't realized that he wasn't alone. Leo took another three steps in silence, each movement slick and calculated.

Almost halfway along the corridor, Leo saw Seth's position clearly for the first time. Seth's arms locked Allissa in place as he dragged her toward apartment 13.

The blood in Leo's veins slowed to the speed of arctic ice. Allissa appeared to be struggling, although Seth held her tight. Just to make sure Allissa couldn't go far, Seth held a blade against her throat.

In less than a heartbeat, Leo assessed the situation. A fission of fear rising through him. He realized if he made a move right now, Seth would end Allissa's life in an instant.

Seth picked up speed, dragging Allissa toward the apartment door that he had planned as the scene of his final kill.

Adrenaline whirred through Leo's veins, and he shook himself into action. His focus narrowed on Seth and Allissa. Fortunately, Allissa's feet kicked and scuffled against the floor, causing enough noise to hide Leo's movements. Seth grunted as Allissa almost struggled free, the knife digging closer to her skin.

For now, Leo figured, it would be better to let Seth and Allissa get into the apartment. Once inside, with no other way out, Seth would be trapped. Seth would also, Leo assumed, release Allissa for a moment to lock the door.

Leo spun around and charged to a fire escape at the end of the corridor. He reached the doorway, turned, and stepped into the recess. Set a few inches in the recess, and at the far end of the gloomy corridor, Leo hoped he would remain out of sight. Leo held his breath, even forcing his chest to become motionless.

Seth dragged Allissa the final few steps down the corridor and reached the door to apartment 13.

Watching Seth twist Allissa around as though she was already lifeless, Leo felt an unusual fear consume his whole being. Leo had never been a violent man in the past, but someone intending to harm Allissa made Leo prepared to do whatever was necessary.

Seth pushed Allissa up against the door and jammed the knife against the back of her neck. Then he released his other hand and removed a key from his pocket.

"Take this," he hissed, forcing the key into Allissa's hand. "Unlock the door."

Allissa took the key with a surprisingly steady hand and slid it into the lock. She turned the key slowly, the old mechanism crunching as the tumblers fell.

Watching silently from less than fifteen feet away, Leo saw Allissa's expression for the first time. Her face was a mask of fear — her eyes wide, and her mouth set into a thin grimace.

The lock mechanism clicked as the key made a full rotation. The door swung forward an inch.

"Good," Seth said, the knife remaining at Allissa's throat throughout. "Push it open."

With the key still in the lock, Allissa extended her hand and shoved the door. The hinges creaked as the door swung open wide and thumped against something inside.

Leo watched, feeling physically sick, as Seth removed the knife from Allissa's neck and shoved her inside.

Seth looked as though he were about to step in after Allissa, then froze. Like a meerkat the first sign of trouble, he glanced back toward the foyer. Then, he turned one hundred and eighty degrees and looked directly at Leo's hiding place.

Leo, barely concealed in the recessed fire escape, panicked. He pushed his back harder into the door. Behind Leo, the fire escape door clunked and swung open. A draft of cold air swept into the corridor. Leo jammed his hands against the frame just in time to prevent himself from falling backward.

Seth swung around and homed in on the noise.

Leo froze, the breath in his lungs turning sour.

Seth tilted his head to the side and stared at the door, fortunately still obscured by the gloom. For what felt like an age, Seth stood motionless and unblinking.

A whining of sirens drifted through the thin window inside the apartment.

As though reminded of his time constraints, Seth turned his attention back to apartment 13. He removed and pocketed the key, then stepped inside and slammed the door.

30

———

ALLISSA STUMBLED forward into the darkened room. Her feet slipped across the floor, and something struck her shin. The pain sent shockwaves through her legs, and she reached out and steadied herself on the wall. An object thumped to the floor, possibly a small table.

Once balanced, Allissa straightened up and turned back to see Seth standing in the doorway. Silhouetted against the light, he cut an imposing figure; his outline, a stark contrast to the brightness behind him. His posture was rigid, the stillness in his frame suggested a predatory focus, and his eyes, though obscured by the back light, bore into something further down the corridor.

Allissa drew a quick breath to focus herself and force away the panic — getting into a state of panic wouldn't help at all. Although Seth was currently blocking the door, and holding a knife, Allissa refused to believe that her fate was sealed.

She cursed herself for not seeing this coming. Now that she considered it, Seth's involvement was obvious. Leo had questioned all along how he knew so much. It was a fact that Niki and Allissa had ignored and now Allissa was into danger.

With a swift, fluid motion, Seth pivoted on his heel and crossed the threshold into the apartment. His gaze fixed on Allissa, with the deliberate, cool precision of a predator zeroing in on its quarry.

Allissa steeled her resolve, refusing to succumb to the role of a victim in waiting. With a fierce determination, she rooted her stance solidly to the ground, and banished the memory of cold steel tracing her flesh. Her every muscle tensed, readying for whatever came next, as she summoned the full force of her will to not become prey in this deadly game.

"I'm so pleased you've decided to join me," Seth said, reaching behind him and slamming the door. His eyes never left Allissa. "Finally, we're alone. I've been waiting for this for a long time."

In one quick move, Seth swung around and locked the door. With the precise movements of a maniac, he removed the key and tucked it back inside his pocket. He switched on the light and looked at Allissa. His eyes were dark, unblinking, and malevolent.

"You freak," Allissa spat.

The piercing wail of sirens filtered through the apartment's flimsy windows. Seth registered the growing clamor with a glance, yet his demeanor remained unsettlingly calm.

Allissa remembered what he'd said to Niki about not planning to get away with this. In fact, he wanted the opposite. He wanted the recognition.

"That's what people will think of you, you know," Allissa said. "They'll call you a freak. They will dig up everything from your past — your school reports, your medical history.

They will poke into everything and pull you apart piece by piece."

Seth's eyes flared as though he were under the influence of strong drugs. "Yes. I will go down in history." He looked hard at Allissa, his gaze boring into her. "People will talk about me for..."

"No, they won't," Allissa said, matching Seth's hard stare with one of her own. Her muscles tensed and a thin film of sweat mottled her brow. It was oppressively warm in the small room. "Well, maybe they'll talk about you for five minutes, using words like *monster* and *madman*."

A shadow of thought swept across Seth's face, but he quickly shook it away.

"Then, everyone will move on to talking about something else, and you'll spend the rest of your sad little life in a cell," Allissa continued. "It's hardly the smartest move." Allissa folded her arms in a gesture of defiance, which appeared much stronger than she felt.

Seth's expression hardened. He paced toward Allissa, raising the knife. "No, no, no," he said, shaking his head as though he were talking to a child. "That's not how it will happen. I know these people and have done so for years. They will talk about me for decades, maybe even centuries."

Allissa shuffled backward, moving slowly, so that Seth didn't immediately lunge at her.

The sirens sounded once more, their insistent wail slicing through the patter of rain against the glass.

"I will be revered, honored, and praised. You will be too. Your sacrifice will be honored for your place in my masterpiece." Seth swept his free hand around the room. "What do you think of the place? This is the place where it all started."

Allissa shuffled backward and glanced around the apartment. It was a simple one-room dwelling which contained a bed with a bare, stained mattress, a small table, and a few cabinets which constituted the kitchen. Allissa assumed that the door to the left led into the bathroom.

"When I learned there was a 13 Miller's Court right here in New York City, I couldn't resist. It's as though it was designed for tonight," Seth said.

Allissa's brow furrowed.

"You haven't worked it out yet!" Seth said, correctly reading her expression. "You don't even know why we're here!" He spat out a laugh.

"All I know, is that I've been kidnapped by a madman and brought to this horrible place," Allissa said, as she pointed to the window through which several sirens howled. "I also know that the police are about to break down that door and lock you up for life."

"Oh, I think we have time. Don't worry about that," Seth said. "There are over one-hundred apartments in the building. They won't even know where to start looking."

Allissa scowled, worried. She'd seen how large the building was from the street and couldn't help but accept that Seth had a point — it would take at least several minutes to find them.

"I've been keeping this place a secret for so long," Seth said, his voice laced with awe. "It's wonderful to share it with someone as extraordinary as you." Seth's eyes moved across Allissa's body.

A wave of repulsion roared through Allissa, although she worked hard to ignore it. She used Seth's momentary distraction to glance around the room once more, searching for something, anything, to use as a weapon.

"You'll be extraordinary once I've finished with you, at least. We're going down in history together."

Allissa noticed a framed picture on the wall behind Seth. It was a large sepia-toned photograph of an eccentric-looking man with a huge mustache.

"Who's that?" Allissa said, pointing at the picture.

The sirens unleashed another mournful howl, their sound growing steadily louder. The noise reminded Allissa that every second she wasted was a small victory.

"That's my great-grandfather," Seth said, his voice was little more than a whisper. Seth stepped forward, closing the distance. "I think you'll be familiar with his work."

Allissa glanced from the photograph to Seth and back again.

"I've never seen him before," she replied defiantly.

Seth ran his free hand through his hair. The knife stayed directed toward Allissa.

"You may know some of his victims," Seth said, before reciting the names from memory. "Mary Ann Nichols, Annie Chapman, Elizabeth Stride, Catherine Eddowes..."

"And Mary Jane Kelly," Allissa interrupted. "Jack the Ripper."

"Clever girl," Seth hissed, sounding genuinely impressed.

"13 Miller's Court," Allissa said, struggling to keep her voice from trembling. "That's where Mary Jane Kelly was murdered."

"Exactly," Seth said. "There's more to it than that, though, 13 Miller's Court was where my great-grandfather could finally fulfill his desires. He had time, and space alone with the victim. What he created was a masterpiece."

"And you think you can do better?" Allissa said. The murders lined up with awful finality in Allissa's mind.

"Not do better," Seth said. "Rather, pay homage."

Seth's words were abruptly severed by a deafening crash that reverberated through the room. The door, previously shut tight, burst open and smashed against the wall.

31

LEO STALKED down the corridor toward apartment 13. He reached the stained door and his eyes narrowed. His muscles rippled with tension. He thought about Allissa inside that room, alone with a man who'd already killed four times in the last few days. Seth had a taste for blood.

Leo took the final few steps on the balls of his feet. He inhaled gently and silently, afraid that any sound right now might reveal his presence.

Rain rattled against the doors of the foyer, beyond which Niki was waiting, and the police were soon to arrive. For a second, Leo considered letting Niki in, but his surging adrenaline reminded him that time was far too short.

Leo leaned toward the door and listened. Seth's muffled voice drifted through the thin wood. Allissa replied and relief swelled through Leo's body — Allissa was still, so far, unharmed.

Although Leo had heard Seth's key grate in the lock, the door looked flimsy. Leo glanced up and down the corridor.

He tried to swallow but couldn't. His mouth tasted dry and metallic.

Leo reeled back, his chest heaving with exertion and eyes ablaze with determination. His palms, slick with a cold sweat, clenched into fists at his sides. He shook his hands, limbering up, rehearsing the critical pivot in his mind. The corridor was silent, a stark contrast to the storm brewing within him. Leo practiced the twisting motion he would need to barge the door with his uninjured shoulder.

Then, in a sudden explosion of energy, Leo lunged forward. Silence forgotten; Leo's feet thundered against the floor. Merely inches away, he spun into a sharp ninety-degree angle, channeling every ounce of strength into his good shoulder.

With a deafening crash, he became a human battering ram; the door buckling under his assault, splinters of wood bursting into the air like fireworks. The door swung open and crashed into the wall; the sound booming through the tiny apartment.

Leo stormed across the threshold. Despite angling his injury away from the impact, pain exploded through Leo's body, threatening to force him into unconsciousness altogether. Leo grabbed hold of the doorjamb to stop himself from falling. He steadied himself quickly and glanced around.

The unexpected clamor caught Seth off-guard. Seth whirled around and swung the knife in Leo's direction. A feral snarl contorted his features, transforming him into the embodiment of menace. Leo easily sidestepped the attack and then knocked Seth's hand away. The knife swung wide, glinting menacingly.

Allissa looked from Seth to Leo. Her eyes were wide with fear. She took two steps backward, creating some distance between herself and the serial killer.

"Are you okay?" Leo said, locking eyes with Allissa for a moment.

"Never better," Allissa replied, shaking the fear from the stance, and standing up straight. "Although I'm fed up with hanging out with this loser." She pointed at Seth.

As Seth recovered his footing, Leo checked out the grim apartment.

"This isn't the way it's supposed to go." Seth took a step backward, raising the knife again. "It doesn't matter. I'll make do."

Leo's hands squeezed into fists as he prepared to take on Seth's attack. It took Leo less than a heartbeat to decide — even if he had to go down with the maniac, Allissa was going to walk away. Leo would stop this killer, even if it cost him everything. He sunk into a crouch and gazed intently into Seth's wild eyes.

Seth locked eyes with Leo, a silent challenge passing between them. With a fluid, almost theatrical flourish, he brandished the knife, its blade slicing an arc through the air. A sinister sneer curled his lips, contorting his face into a mask of malice.

"Drop the knife," Leo said, edging toward Allissa. "Your fun is over."

In a sudden pivot, Seth's body coiled and unleashed like a spring. He lunged toward Allissa, the knife a silver flash in his hand, zigzagging with precision.

Leo turned, charged across the room, and grabbed the framed photograph from the wall. The photograph wasn't much of a weapon, but the frame looked heavy, and it was better than taking on Seth bare handed.

Leo tore the picture from its fixing and whirled back toward Seth.

Six feet away, Seth closed in on Allissa. Seth swept the

knife in a wide arc toward Allissa's neck. Seeing the strike, Allissa backed away. Seth lunged forward again. His eyes shone with manic determination. He feigned a stabbing motion with the knife, causing Allissa to dodge to the right. Seth swung in the same direction as Allissa and grabbed a fist full of her hair. Seth held the knife high. His muscles tensed for the downward stroke.

Allissa screamed and lashed out like a writhing ball of energy.

Seth pulled Allissa's hair harder. Allissa kicked out, landing several heavy blows on Seth's legs. Wholly focused on finishing the job, Seth didn't even flinch. Seth yanked on the hair, pulling Allissa's head backward and exposing her throat.

Allissa delivered two punches to Seth's midriff.

Seth's jaw clenched. His muscles tightened. The knife swung through the air, approaching Allissa's neck.

Leo, his shoulder aflame with searing agony, propelled himself across the room. Every fiber of his being burned with pain. He hoisted the heavy frame, muscles screaming in protest. With his adversary in sight, he surged forward, and with a Herculean effort, swung the frame toward Seth's outstretched arm.

Seth's knife swept down. It was just inches from Allissa's exposed throat now. Allissa cried out and tried to move. Seth pulled her hair even harder. Allissa struck him in the chin and again in the stomach. He didn't even blink.

Seth's blade descended in a merciless arc, glinting malevolently as it moved. The razor's edge hovered mere breaths away from Allissa's flesh.

Allissa howled, a desperate plea as she twisted violently under his iron grip. With primal ferocity, Allissa sent a fist into Seth's jaw. His lip split and blood oozed across his face.

Allissa twisted in the other direction and sent another strike deep into Seth's stomach.

The frame crashed into Seth's forearm with a thunderous splintering of wood and bone. The glass within the frame shattered, flying through the room like raindrops. Seth's eyes, wide with shock, snapped shut as a raw, visceral howl ripped from his throat. His arm contorted to an unnatural angle, and the knife spun from his grip.

A guttural scream tore through the room as Seth's gaze reopened to the harsh reality of his mangled limb. Releasing Allissa's hair, he cradled his shattered arm, his face a twisted canvas of agony and disbelief.

The knife clanged to the floor and spun under the bed.

Gathering every ounce of his resolve, Leo reared back. With a warrior's precision, he swung the frame again. The frame met the back of Seth's skull with a dull, sickening thud. Seth's legs buckled beneath him, sending him crumpling to the floor.

Leo, his chest heaving with the exertion of survival, stood over Seth. His eyes blazed with fierce determination, ready to bring down the final, crushing blow. Leo poised himself to strike, to end this horror once and for all.

"No, no, stop," Allissa said, grabbing Leo's arm. "Let the police finish this."

Feeling Allissa's touch, Leo's anger dissipated almost immediately. He dropped the frame, and then crouched over Seth, and pinned him to the floor. Seth flailed about, trying to shake Leo off. Leo grabbed Seth's uninjured arm and pushed it up behind his back.

"My arm, my arm!" Seth shouted.

"I'll break the other one too," Leo snarled.

"Hey, look at that," Allissa said, pointing to the wall where the picture had been.

There was a hollow in the wall and some items were stashed inside.

"Touch that and I'll kill you," Seth said, writhing more frantically now.

Leo pushed Seth's arm higher behind his back.

Allissa crossed the room and pulled the items from the hollow. She dropped them onto the bed. There was a thick roll of banknotes and a passport.

"Where were you going?" Allissa said, picking up the passport. She looked at Leo and her expression melted into a smile.

"What's happening?" came a voice from the door. Niki charged into the room, followed by a pair of police officers.

Seth lashed out and tried to stand. Leo pushed Seth's head against the floor.

The red and blue lights of two more police cars strobed through the thin curtains. The noise of more sirens slicing through the rain.

"You've got him!" Niki said, turning to the officers. "I think you'll find this is the Downtown Ripper." She pointed at Seth, who was lashing about on the floor.

"That's him alright," Allissa said. As the officers moved in to make the arrest, Allissa casually slipped the roll of banknotes into her pocket.

Leo released Seth and let the officers take control. He crossed the room and hugged Allissa. Then, after looking back at Seth, he eyed Niki and then Allissa. "I told you he was dangerous," Leo said, finally taking a breath.

32

"Where were you when this happened?" Allissa asked. "Do you remember?"

"Yes, I do," Leo said. "I was on the bus on the way back from school. The radio was on, and it was all over the news. I didn't really understand what was happening until I got home and saw it on the telly."

Allissa stepped up to the railing of the 9/11 Memorial in Lower Manhattan. She peered down at the pool that marked the location of where the North Tower once stood. Water trickled down the sides, giving the pools an impression of infinity. The railings surrounding the pools displayed the names of those who lost their lives on that fateful day.

Leo glanced up at the people, most wrapped in thick coats and scarves, against the winter chill. Some read the names, and others gazed at the sky. A group of school children in matching red hats followed their teacher toward the South Tower.

"How do you feel about going home?" Leo asked. "We were lucky to get those flights tomorrow."

Two days had passed since Seth's arrest. After giving their statements to the police, and being checked over by medics, Leo and Allissa returned to their hotel room, where they'd caught up on a sleepless night. After the day's harrowing events, Allissa had doubted she'd be able to relax. In the comfort of her bed in their hotel, however, she sunk quickly into deep and luscious sleep. She knew the memory of the cold steel against her throat would live on, but she also knew that without what she, Leo, and Niki, had done, a killer would have remained at large.

They'd been awakened by Leo's ringing phone. Emma was frantic and emotional when she told them Andy had been immediately released with all charges dropped. It seemed with everything else going on, the NYPD weren't that interested in finding out how the Porsche ended up trashed in the Lincoln Tunnel.

"Yeah. I'm excited about it," Allissa said, gazing across the pool. "When we get home, we're having some time off. I don't care what comes up." She ran a gloved hand across her throat.

"For sure," Leo said. "With the money that Seth kindly donated, we can have at least a couple of weeks off."

Leo and Allissa had split the money they'd found behind the picture in apartment 13. They'd given some to Michael to help clear Andy's debt and split the remainder between themselves and Niki. Niki said that she would pass a few hundred dollars on to Axel to help New York's homeless population, without whom they wouldn't have solved the case.

"When are Andy and Emma flying home?" Allissa asked.

"They're going to stay another few days, I think," Leo said, turning his attention to people milling around on the other side of the memorial. "They're still determined to salvage something of a holiday, what with Andy being in jail for the last few days."

"Yeah, that's not exactly the getaway they'd hoped for," Allissa said.

"Let's hope it's taught him something. Now he's got the opportunity to do what's right for Emma and Frankie," Leo said, thinking out loud. "If he just fills himself with booze again, there will be trouble."

"And with you being the sort of guy who takes down serial killers, Andy really should pay attention," Allissa said, leaning against Leo's shoulder.

"Exactly." Leo threw Allissa a glance. "There's clearly no knowing the limits of my physical prowess."

Allissa laughed and then added, "Andy did say that he wouldn't drink again."

"Yes, he did say that," Leo agreed, "and that's a great start. I just hope he can actually do it."

Allissa nodded. "Maybe we should stay in England for a couple of months just to keep an eye on them."

"I'd like that, actually."

Leo and Allissa took a step back to let an older couple pass. The couple read each of the names and then paused for a moment before moving on to the next.

"Hey, look who it is." Allissa pointed across the pool.

Leo followed Allissa's gaze and saw Niki Zadid standing at the railing, her blue headscarf trembling in the breeze. She placed her hands on one of the names and whispered something. Then, as quickly as she appeared, she turned and walked away.

"Come on," Allissa said, "let's go and see…"

Leo was about to argue, but Allissa had already slipped away through the crowd.

Allissa reached the point where Niki had been standing and scanned the names.

"My husband," came a voice from behind them. Leo and Allissa spun to see Niki behind them. "We'd only been married six months, then this happened." Niki stepped between Leo and Allissa and touched one of the inscribed names.

"I'm sorry, I had no idea," Allissa said.

"Why would you?" Niki locked eyes with Allissa for a long moment. "He'd only been working here a few months." Niki dabbed at her eyes, then disguised it by straightening her headscarf. "It's just one of those things. I was studying law at the time, but soon after qualifying, I realized my heart just wasn't in it. I needed to do something different, something for me."

Niki spun around and led them away from the memorial. She stopped and glanced from Allissa to Leo and back again. "It's a reminder to make sure you're not wasting time, as you never know what's coming. If there's something you gotta do, then you gotta do it."

Leo gazed into Niki's eyes. Allissa nodded.

"When are you guys off?" Niki asked, her voice lightening as her lopsided smile returned.

"Tomorrow," Allissa said.

Leo stood in silence. The words Niki had said to him in their private conversation a few days ago, tumbled through his mind.

"Oh gosh, tomorrow?" Niki said, dissolving back into her larger-than-life persona. "Well, you've got loads to see. You don't wanna waste your time chatting here. Where you heading?"

"Not sure," Leo said, "we've heard the High Line's worth a visit."

"Sure is," Niki said. "It's a bit of a walk, but for you young things, that'll be fine. Head that way and just keep going."

"Thanks," Leo said, "and thanks for your help finding Andy."

"Anytime," Niki said, "and thanks for your help catching the killer. With all the news interest, I think it's going to be good for business."

"Happy to help," Leo said.

"If you're ever back over here, look me up for sure," Niki said.

"We will," Allissa said, pulling Niki into a hug.

The women remained locked for a few seconds and then separated. Allissa turned and started in the direction Niki had indicated.

Leo and Niki stared at each other.

"Do it," Niki whispered, an additional glimmer in her eyes.

"I will," Leo mouthed in reply. Forcing a nervous smile, he hurried after Allissa.

The afternoon was getting colder now. People rushed with their collars turned up against the chill. Leo and Allissa walked in silence for a few minutes.

"This place reminds me of that night in St Lucia," Allissa said, glancing up at Leo beside her.

"Why?"

"That night, after escaping through the party, we were talking about how sometimes all this feels like a film. It really feels like it, walking around here. Don't you think?"

"I suppose," Leo agreed.

"You never answered my question that night, either."

Leo couldn't remember the question.

"If our lives were a film, who would play you?" Allissa tapped Leo on the arm.

Leo inhaled the cool winter air. He let the air fill his lungs, feed his courage, then let it go slowly. He gazed at the surrounding buildings, then turned to Allissa.

Their hands fell together like the last leaves of fall.

"Who would play me?" Leo looked down at the woman he'd literally followed to the ends of the earth. He paused, remembering how he'd been so afraid to lose her. Now, he couldn't even imagine their lives apart.

In his mind's eye, the final scene of a movie played out — strings rose to their climax, the camera zoomed out, and dust danced in the projector's beam.

"I'd play me," Leo said, moving his hand to Allissa's waist. "If you promised to play you."

As Leo leaned forward, the world around them held its breath. A hush descended across the street — a profound stillness that felt as though time itself had slowed in recognition of what was to come. Then, the sky joined in the silent ovation, releasing the first gentle flakes of winter. The snowflakes swirled around the towering silhouettes of the surrounding towers, dancing and weaving their way toward Leo and Allissa as they embraced.

Leo didn't notice any of this as he bent down and placed his lips against Allissa's. Deep inside him, a silent storm of emotion erupted, releasing all the tension and longing that had been building between them. The softness of Allissa's lips was the final piece to a puzzle he hadn't known he was assembling, a missing harmony in a symphony of survival. As their lips met, a gentle yet fierce warmth spread through them, a silent promise that no matter what had passed or what was to come, this connection, this perfect now, was theirs to keep.

Niki Zadid peered out from behind a building and looked straight at Leo and Allissa. True to form, curiosity had got the better of her and she'd followed them at a discreet distance, wanting to see if Leo was a man of his word. As the couple locked in a kiss which she knew had been a long time coming, Niki smiled her lopsided smile.

"My work here is done," she said to herself, before straightening her headscarf, turning on her heels, and walking toward Greenwich Village.

Andreja Panasenko thought she knew her mother. But then, death changes everything.

To avoid losing her inheritance, Andreja must reconnect with her estranged sister. One problem, her sister went missing as a child, nearly fifty years ago.

Leo & Allissa travel to Riga to help, but they're barely off the plane before Andreja's nowhere to be seen. Taken or fled, they don't know, but to find her, they must follow clues dating back to a time when powerful men ruled supreme.

From the backstreets of Riga to the vast Latvian forests,

Leo & Allissa stumble into a dog-eat-dog world of politics, lies and secrets. Can they find the truth about a woman who hasn't been seen in fifty years, or will the ghosts of the past get the final word?

Riga is the new international detective thriller from bestselling author, Luke Richardson. If you like Clive Cussler, Nick Thacker, Ernest Dempsey, and Russell Blake, then you'll love this explosive new adventure.

Search your local Amazon store, your favourite bookseller, or ask in your library for **Riga Rising by Luke Richardson.**
www.lukerichardsonauthor.com/riga

A dream proposal turns into a heart-stopping nightmare when Leo's fiancée vanishes without a trace in the tropical paradise of Koh Tao.

Travelling the world with the love of his life, Leo's looking for the perfect place to propose. Reaching the Thai tropical paradise of Koh Tao, he thinks he's found it.

But before he gets an answer, she's nowhere to be seen.

On searching the resort, his tranquillity turns to turmoil. What began as a dream escape swiftly spirals into a harrowing quest as he must to work out whether this is a practical joke gone wrong, or something much more sinister.

Discover where it all began in KOH TAO BETRAYAL, the compelling introduction to Luke Richardson's Best-selling International Detective Series.

Grab your FREE copy now!
www.lukerichardsonauthor.com/kohtao

AUTHOR'S NOTE

Once again, thank you for joining me for another adventure. I hope you enjoyed the story. Before writing this book, many readers had asked me whether Leo and Allissa would ever get together. Of course, I answered how all writers do when asked questions like that... you'll have you wait and find out.

In truth, we don't answer like in that way to be obtuse, we often genuinely don't know how the story and the relationship between our characters are going to play out. I was confident that my two main characters' relationship would turn into a romantic one, but I just wasn't sure when and how. Then, as I was writing that final scene at the 911 memorial in Manhattan, it just felt right.

I particularly loved writing the character of Niki Zadid in this story. I feel like she's got countless interesting stories to tell of her own, and maybe at some point in the future I'll get to write them. New York is, after all, a city with a dark side, and I think Niki Zadid would be a totally new take on the classic P.I. to investigate it.

I visited New York in 2018 on the return journey from my brother's wedding in the St Lucia—where the opening parts to this novel are set. It seemed logical to me that Leo and Allissa share my trip, although mine was far less dramatic (thankfully). I've yet to return to either New York or St Lucia, but know I will.

As a fan of jazz music, I loved featuring the Opus Club in this story. While the club itself is fictional, it's based on several I visited during my time there. New York City has been a hub for jazz music since the early 20th century, playing a particularly significant role in the development and popularization of the genre. In the 1920s and 1930s, speakeasies and clubs in Harlem, such as the Cotton Club and the Savoy Ballroom, became renowned for their jazz performances, featuring legendary artists like Duke Ellington, Ella Fitzgerald, and Billie Holiday.

However, it was in the 1940s and 1950s that the Village in Lower Manhattan, where much of this story is set, emerged as the epicenter of the jazz scene. Clubs like the Village Vanguard, Blue Note, and Cafe Society showcased the talents of iconic musicians such as Charlie Parker, Thelonious Monk, Miles Davis, and John Coltrane. These intimate venues provided a platform for experimentation and collaboration, allowing artists to push the boundaries of the genre and create new styles like bebop and hard bop.

It's wonderful to still be able to visit these venues. The music, the clubs, and the characters who inhabited them offer endless possibilities for exploration and imagination.

Seth Stryker's great grandfather, accused of the Jack the Ripper murders, was based on a real person. Francis Tumblety is a name that I'm surprised hasn't featured in more modern media. An Irish-American, Tumblety was a quack doctor, con man, and a suspect in the notorious Jack the Ripper murders that terrorized London in 1888. Born in Ireland, Tumblety immigrated to the United States as a young man and began a career as a self-proclaimed physician, selling dubious medicines and performing illegal operations.

Tumblety was known for his flamboyant personality, often dressing in extravagant clothing and sporting a large handlebar mustache. He claimed to have served as a surgeon in the Union Army during the American Civil War, although this has never been substantiated.

In 1888, Tumblety was in London during the time of the Jack the Ripper murders. His reputation as a misogynist and his alleged connections to the sex trade in the city's East End made him a person of interest to the police. Tumblety was arrested on charges of gross indecency and was released on bail. He fled to France and later returned to the United States, evading further questioning by Scotland Yard.

While Tumblety was never formally charged with the Jack the Ripper murders, he remains one of the most intriguing suspects in the case. Some researchers have pointed to his medical background, his hatred of women, and his presence in London during the murders as evidence of his potential guilt. Others, however, argue that the evidence against him is largely circumstantial and that he was just one of many suspects investigated by the police.

After returning to the United States, Tumblety continued his career as a quack doctor, traveling across the country and selling his remedies. He was arrested several times for various offenses, including selling obscene literature and running a brothel.

In his later years, Tumblety lived in St. Louis, Missouri, where he died in 1903. He left behind a complicated legacy, with some remembering him as a charming and eccentric figure, while others saw him as a dangerous criminal and a potential serial killer. Whatever he was, the mysteries surrounding him has fascinated researchers and true crime enthusiasts for over a century. Also, his life story offers a glimpse into the dark underbelly of Victorian society and the enduring allure of one of history's most notorious unsolved crimes.

Once again, although the words here are my own, the characters, experiences and some of the events described are wholly inspired by the people I've traveled beside.

If we ever shared noodles from a street-food vendor, visited a temple together, played cards on a creaking overnight train, or had a beer in a back-street restaurant, you are forever in this book, and for that, I thank you too!

Again, thank you for coming on the adventure with me. I hope to see you again.

Luke

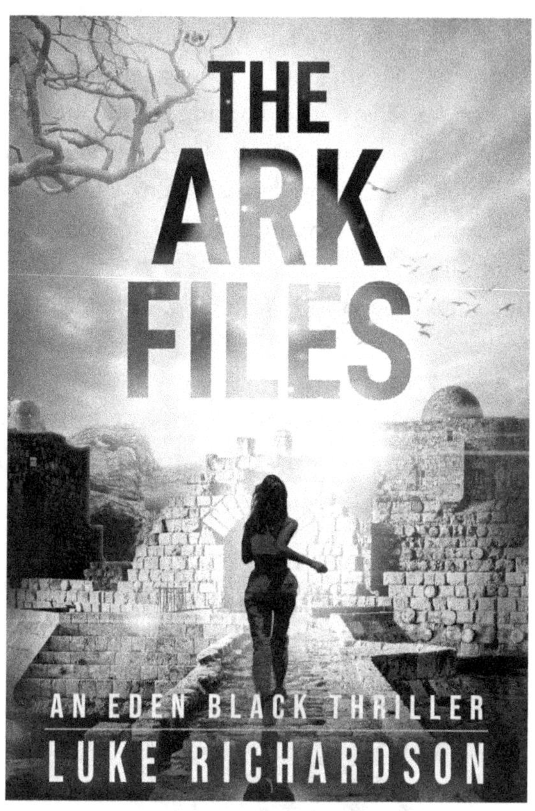

A secret society...
An ancient manuscript...
One woman to save the world...

Professional treasure hunter EDEN BLACK is no stranger to action. After all, the artifacts she spends her life returning to their rightful owners aren't always easy to access.

When Eden's father dies in a plane crash, her life's turned upside down. Grief turns to fear when she learns that it wasn't an accident. Everyone involved in an archaeological dig twenty years ago has met with a similar untimely end. Everyone that is, but Eden who was ten at the time.

When her father's house is raided and burned to the ground, Eden's forced into action. To learn the truth about her father's death and save herself from sharing his fate, Eden must uncover the manuscript and expose its secrets once and for all.

But this time the world is watching, and not everyone is on her side.

THE ARK FILES is the first in a brand-new pulse-pounding archaeological thriller series by Luke Richardson. Fans of Dan Brown, Clive Cussler, and Ernest Dempsey will devour this in hours!

www.lukerichardsonauthor.com/arkfiles

Or search your local Amazon store, your favourite bookseller, or ask in your local library for **The Ark Files by Luke Richardson.**